Felix

The Extraordinary Tale of an Extraordinary Cat

Felix

The Extraordinary Tale
of an Extraordinary Cat

The first of a trilogy of stories

by

Margaret Rice

Illustrated by
Geoffrey Phillips

ISBN 978-0-9569998-0-1

Printed and bound in the UK by
MPG Books Group, Bodmin and King's Lynn

First published in the UK in 2011 by

TDF Publishing
Sleaford, Lincolnshire

In loving memory of

Felix

and his

family and friends

The Story of

Felix and Other Cats,

A Fat Boxer,

Fionn and Other Great Danes

Dedicated to:

Daisy Boxer and Great Danes, Charlie and Fionn,
whose tolerance of having their home invaded by
a succession of uninvited cats was exemplary.

Also my first teacher, Kathleen Walker,
for stimulating my interest in the written word,

and Jan & Haydn Wesley, without whose
encouragement it is doubtful this tale
ever would have been told.

Contents

Part One

New Beginnings

It was a cold, wet and windy night, and the two sisters huddled together in a ditch, shivering.

Grey Cat looked anxiously at her sister, White Cat, and said, 'You know, if we don't find somewhere soon, we're not going to make it.'

They looked at each other solemnly and, in their misery of fear and despondency, they thought of their mother and began remembering how comfortable life had once been for them.

Then they thought of Horace, the astonishingly handsome cat, who was always so meticulously turned out in his finest, carefully groomed coat of white, figured with glossy jet black patches.

When first they had met him, he had told them that, after a life of servitude, he was now 'an independent' and not attached to any human household, but that there was a place he visited, when in need. A place where there was always a warm bed and food waiting for him, or any other lonely traveller in need.

To the two girls, who at the time were not faring well as 'independents', this haven had sounded like a paradise on earth.

White Cat's mouth had watered at the persistent mental

picture of all the succulent food which awaited hungry cats at such a place.

When asked where was it this place existed, Horace (a name he said had been given to him by Abe and Cara, the people who fed him, and was one which he was happy to accept and use) would wave a front paw in the general direction from whence he had come and vaguely refer to various landmarks along the way to it.

The girls had listened intently to what he had had to say – the long stone wall which led to the top of a hill, the big tree at the top, and how it was necessary to travel with the warm sun in your eyes in the morning, as, if you waited until later in the day, the sun deliberately led you in the opposite direction.

Whenever they had happened upon Horace, although too shy, and ashamed, to admit to him that they were in need, they tried always to turn the conversation to 'The Bothy' as he called it, but often elicited no more detail from him. Sometimes he would be in a hurry with urgent business to attend to, and only social pleasantries could be exchanged, and on other occasions he would be intent upon knowing more about the sisters and their lives.

Foolishly, they had continued to convey the impression to Horace that all was well with them, and they wanted for nothing.

In fact, at the time they had first met Horace, they were tired of scavenging in dustbins and picking up small dead crabs from the beach, onto which a violent sea in wild winter storms had flung them. With their hard shells, the splintered bits of which caught in the teeth, they tasted dreadful. The small amount which was edible always was already decaying, and that, mixed with a liberal helping of sea debris, sand and gravel, made for a meagre and very depressing meal.

Back in the present, the sisters' thoughts turned to their kittenhood, when their first memories of life were the warm embrace at their mother's breast, and of suckling her sweet, warm milk.

They sighed deeply. They turned to each other and vowed silently to stick together and face whatever destiny had in store for them now.

Lizzie

The mother of Grey Cat and White Cat was born on the farm of a very kindly man, who set the well-being of his animals above his profits.

Even those who were long past earning their keep kept their home with him.

Take Lizzie's Aunt Carmel for instance. She had lost her sight years ago and there was no way she could help to keep the rodents away from the animal feed, but the farmer always had a kind word for her too when he came each day to feed them.

Lizzie was happy and content on the farm, but she succumbed to the reality of the old adage that 'curiosity killed the cat'.

Admittedly it didn't actually kill her, but it did change her life for ever.

Her little brothers and sisters were content to suckle and then sleep most of the day away, but she (the youngest and smallest kitten) was different, always busying herself around the barn and yard.

She kept herself occupied all day, toddling along on her fat little legs, investigating everything.

The farmer looked on in amusement.

One day, when she was still very small, the farmer came

into the barn, where she and her siblings were snuggled up to their mother.

He leaned down, and, singling her out, rolled her over and tickled her tubby little tummy. She squeaked her delight.

'Well, my busy little friend, I think you shall be "Lizzie",' he said, and, turning to her mother, 'What do you think, Annie?' Her mother purred her approval. 'Then, Lizzie it is.'

The days passed. Lizzie grew stronger and developed her climbing skills, and soon there was nowhere in the barn which she hadn't reached and investigated, and she knew every inch of the yard outside.

She would have to go further afield to satisfy her curiosity.

There was *one* thing she had not yet had the confidence to investigate. It was a curious object, which appeared and disappeared on most days, in the company of Mary, the farmer's daughter.

Mary would come out of the house, open one of the object's wings, sit behind the object's head and close the wing again. Next the object would make a loud noise, and then away it would go, with Mary.

Later on in the day, the object would return. It would be back where it was earlier, the noise would stop, the wing open, Mary get out, and then she would close the wing again, before walking away from the object, to go back up to the house.

What was it?
What did it do?
What was it for?
She *had* to find out.

Horace

Down on the farm, Horace was busy with his chores. Although no longer young, he was still strikingly handsome, but, just at this time though, his snowy white coat, with its glossy jet black patches, was decorated in dust and cobwebs, as he pushed his way in and out of all the nooks and crannies of the old barn, seeking out the hiding places of his adversaries – the rats and mice who devoted themselves to trying to get through his defences, in order to feast on the cattle feed, which it was his job to protect.

Horace was born and raised on the farm and his job now was the same as it had always been – to scare away the rats and mice from the cattle feed and root vegetables stored in the old leaky barn which was his home.

His own rations were meagre enough and Horace couldn't remember a time when he hadn't been hungry, but it had always been so and he accepted it without question.

The brothers who owned the farm were as nasty a pair as anyone would find, anywhere. They were dirty, lazy, dishonest, deceitful, neglectful, and cruel. They were a disgrace to the supposedly intelligent species to which they belonged.

Except for hair colouring, the brothers were almost identical in their appearance and in their habits.

The very slightly shorter of the two had a shock of bright red curly hair, and the other one, black and straight.

Both were thick-set in stature, and had small, cruel eyes, set in fat florid faces, above thick necks, sloping shoulders, and thick fleshy arms. Their bulging 'beer' bellies drooped down over short, bandy legs.

Their bodies and clothes were grimed with dirt, and both always smelt very strongly of drink and cigarette smoke.

The smell of beer and smoke was offensive to Horace's nostrils, causing him to wrinkle his nose, and snuffle and cough repeatedly, whenever in the presence of either of them.

BroBlack saw himself as being in charge, and BroRed was happy to go along with that notion, because, when things went wrong on the farm, as they frequently did, he could absolve himself from blame by whingeing on that he did not make the decisions.

It had never occurred to Horace to question why the two brothers were so fat from all the food they ate themselves, while they gave so little to him and to the other animals on the farm. He had always been lean, but, as he got older, he had noticed his meals had been getting smaller and smaller, and he was losing weight all the time.

While he continued to take pride in his appearance, as he groomed his coat each day, he became more and more worried at the ease with which the hairs came away from his skin, and to see how slack his coat was becoming on his body.

He had never had the benefit of a good diet, or of veterinary care for his ills, but, somehow or other, he had always managed to shake off any sickness which had beset him.

However now, in his circumstances, he was finding it hard to cope with the difficulties of approaching old age. Life in a leaky, draughty barn had taken its toll of his health and, each day, his limbs felt stiffer and the joints more painful.

Horace knew his eyesight and hearing were not what they used to be and neither was he as nimble now as the job demanded. Although he remained vigilant, as always, at his post to repel the rodent invaders, try as he might, some always managed to slip past him to help themselves to the feed and the vegetables.

When the brothers came into the barn each day to collect the cattle's meagre rations – which were barely enough to keep them from starving – they would shout and swear when they saw the damage.

Horace would advance to try to explain that he was too old now to cope on his own, and he needed help on Rodent Duty, but the shouts and oaths then would be directed at him, closely followed by any missile near at hand. On one such occasion, Horace had narrowly escaped serious injury when a pitchfork had been thrown at him.

One morning, when, to try to drive away the pangs of hunger from his stomach and his thoughts, Horace was trying to doze in a shaft of sunlight coming in through the open door of the hayloft, one of the brothers strode in.

Horace rose to greet him, nervously edging towards the man, purring.

This morning, BroRed seemed to be in better humour, because, instead of inspecting the feed and vegetables, and then losing his temper, he made for Horace, hand extended with a tasty titbit in it.

Horace took the titbit gratefully and thought that, at last, the brothers had understood that the damage to the feed and vegetables was not his fault. Maybe now they would get him some help. A youngster would do, one whom he could train for Rodent Duty.

He was just thinking how good it would be to have a companion to help him, when he was startled to be suddenly grasped by the scruff of his neck and thrust roughly into a box, and the lid closed on him. 'Time for you to go,' said the man.

'Go, go where?' thought Horace briefly, before all his attention needed to be directed into trying to keep his feet while the box was swayed around as it was carried away. Next, the box stopped swaying and was set down, and Horace heard the engine of the brothers' battered old vehicle leap into life.

A short, bumpy ride then followed, before the box was picked up and began swaying again.

Poor Horace felt giddy and quite sick from the movement and from the stifling heat beginning to build up inside the box from the lack of any ventilation.

Next, the box was set down again, the lid opened, and Horace saw he was on the foreshore of the beach, not too far from his home.

Before he could jump out, the man knotted a length of twine tightly around his neck and then pulled him roughly from the box.

Horace stood there, beside the box, waiting for instructions, but none came.

The man ignored him and busied himself looping the

other end of the twine around a large boulder nearby on the beach. Then, without speaking to Horace, looking at him, or looking back, the man picked up the empty box, strode off and soon was out of sight.

Horace sat down, and then just sat there. He was puzzled. Why had he been brought here, and what was expected of him?

There were no rats or mice around here, and, even if there had been, with his movements being restricted to the length of the twine attached to him, he couldn't chase them off anyway.

Horace thought, and thought, but just couldn't make it out.

At length, he gave up trying to find an answer, and allowed the warmth of the Spring sunshine on the pebbles, and the sound of the lapping waves, to take over and lull him into a deep sleep.

Horace awoke very suddenly – as the first wave to reach him on the incoming tide went right over him, dousing him in icy cold water. He coughed and spluttered and scrambled to his feet – just as the next wave hit him, knocked him down, and then went over him too.

Horace realized he was in serious trouble. Obviously the farmer had forgotten to come back for him in time, and, tied to a boulder as he was, he would be unable to swim ashore to save himself from drowning.

Although he had always accepted as their absolute right whatever the brothers did, or did not do, a desperate situation called for drastic action.

He was ready for the next wave, taking a deep breath, and bracing himself against its force.

As it receded again, he moved towards the boulder, a little higher up the beach, where he then took up a section of his tether into his mouth and clawed and gnawed at it, all the while watching for the next wave. Just before each wave reached him, he took a deep breath and held onto the boulder as the wave washed over him.

The water was under his chin by the time the last strand of the twine broke under the frantic assault of his claws and teeth, and he was able to drag his sodden, exhausted body clear of the water and up to the top of the beach, out of the reach of the waves. He lay there for a long time, and dusk was deepening by the time he had the strength to stand up and head for home.

As he arrived back at the farm, with the broken end of the twine still dangling from the tight loop around his neck, he saw that the brother who had taken him to the beach that morning was crossing the yard.

Horace ran forward, whereupon the man swore and called to his brother, 'You'll never believe it, that useless old cat has got free and has come back.'

His brother ran from the house, shouting, 'Well, don't just stand there, chase him off, there's no place here for any who don't earn their keep.'

'*Don't earn their keep*,' thought Horace, 'What keep, and how can they say that about *me*? I've given them years and years of loyal service and I can't help getting old.'

He was so astonished, he just stood there.

'Ouch.' yelped Horace, as the first stone hit him on the flank with a stinging blow. He turned to look and saw blood oozing out of a deep cut, staining the white hair of his coat around the wound crimson red. Just at that moment, another stone found its target, hitting Horace hard just below one ear.

He turned back to look at the brothers, and saw that they were picking up stones off the yard and hurling them at him.

As they continued to pelt him with stones, poor Horace turned and fled.

Once out of sight, in the safety of the bushes on the hillside overlooking the farm, Horace sat down and tried to make sense of the day's events.

After lengthy deliberation, he concluded that leaving him on the beach had *not* been a mistake. It had been deliberate. They didn't want him any more and so had tried to kill him.

Although they had never shown him any care or affection, in Horace's eyes he had been born into the brothers' service and therefore he had always done his duty to the best of his ability, in the belief that his loyalty lay with them.

The tears sprang into his eyes with the hurt he felt about the way they had thought of him and had treated him. They had tried to drown him, and, when that had failed, they had driven him off from his home – the only home he had ever known.

While the overwhelming emotion for Horace was one of hurt, he felt foolish too: After what had happened to his mother, he should have been more wary around the brothers when he himself was becoming old, and they were becoming less and less satisfied with his services.

To desert his post was unthinkable of course, but he

should have been alert to the signs they actually meant him serious harm.

Horace's thoughts returned to his mother, and of how much he had loved her. She had been so sweet and kind to him and he had adored her. He felt a warm glow in his heart whenever her dear face came to mind.

His face clouded, he frowned, and a tear came to his eye, as he remembered how cruelly one of the brothers had treated her when she fell ill.

She had been sick for several days, too weak to rise from her bed, but, until that fateful stormy evening, fortunately she had not been noticed, as she lay there uncomplaining, in a corner of the barn.

That evening, one of the brothers came into the barn and saw her.

Horace and his mother had trembled, when they saw he was much the worse for drink. 'Why are you lying around, idle?' he had roared at Horace's mother.

Then, starting across the barn towards her, staggering from side to side, again in his loud, slurred voice, he had demanded, 'What's the matter with you?'

Horace's mother was terrified, but, too weak to stand, all she could do was to cower there, shivering with fever and with fear.

Horace saw he meant her harm and had tried to intervene, by weaving in and out of the brother's feet to distract him and slow him down, but the man had leaned down and grabbed him by the scruff of his neck, then turned around unsteadily, and thrown him hard against the barn door.

Horace had slumped into a heap, whimpering in pain, and was so dazed he couldn't get up and on to his feet.

Horace heard the brother shout at his mother, 'There's no room here for slackers, so get up, or it'll be the worse for you.'

His mother was unable to move, and, with his head still spinning, Horace saw her pleading for mercy with her huge, solemn eyes, in a face pinched with pain.

Then, to his horror, he saw the man grab his dear, defenceless mother by the scruff of her neck and, with her whimpering weakly as she dangled helplessly in his grasp, carry her back across the barn and throw her out of the door into the wind and rain.

Horace knew that, in her weakened state, his mother would die out there, and he managed to half scramble to his feet, to try to dodge the brother and get outside to his mother before the door closed. A kick to his ribs sent him reeling back into the barn and then the door had slammed shut.

All that night Horace heard the wind howling around the barn, and the torrential rain beating down on to the roof, as he tried desperately to find a way out to go to his mother's side, but all was tightly closed and locked.

As morning dawned, and the wind and rain abated, Horace sat anxiously by the barn door, awaiting his chance to escape to find his mother.

It was mid-morning before his chance came.

The sun was shining again, and the birds singing, when the other brother opened the door to come in, and Horace slipped through and was gone.

He did not have to search far for his mother. He found her lying, face down, in the long grass to one side of the barn, where she had fallen when the other brother had thrown her out the night before. Her coat was sodden and muddy, and she was deathly still.

As soon as Horace touched her, he knew the worst, his dearest mother was dead.

The tears for her flowed down his cheeks as he crouched beside her still, lifeless body and laid his head against her. He wished her a speedy journey into the care of their Lord Provider; he thanked her for the happiness of his kittenhood in her care, and for her unerring love and wisdom. He promised her he would live his life according to the standards she had set for him, and, in all things, he would be the son she had striven so hard to bring up correctly.

He told her he was sorry he had failed to protect her.

It was sunset before Horace rose to go. He touched her again lightly to say goodbye and then, with one lingering backward glance to the one cat in the world he had loved above any other, he returned to his duties, and to keep his promises to his mother.

He couldn't have known that as he kept his vigil by her lifeless earthly body, his mother had been smiling down upon him as she watched her dear son grieving for her, beside the body she had left long before he had found it.

She had longed to be able to speak to him, to touch him, and to reassure him that all was now well with her, but that was not in the way of things, and she knew she had to content herself in the knowledge that she could stay close by him, to watch over him throughout his earthly life, until the time came for him to embark on his journey, and they could be together again.

Although, as she had lain dying, it had angered her to think of the brother who had shown her no mercy in her distress, she had since forgiven both brothers for their long mistreatment of her, and her beloved son, knowing for certain now that one day each would be shown the error of his ways, and would learn to rue a misspent earthly life and cruel ill-treatment of his fellow creatures.

She had accepted it was not her place to judge them.

Back in the present, Horace thought on for a while about all the years of his life he had spent there, at the brothers' farm, always hungry, but nonetheless determined to carry on.

The only times he had ever had to escape the dreary monotony of his life of drudgery on the farm had been on those occasions when he was called upon to take his place as feline co-opted member at sessions of the Country Creatures Code of Conduct Committee (the C.C.C.C.C.), and, even then, having slipped away silently from the barn, he remained anxious all of the time to get back home as quickly as possible, before he was missed and the brothers thought he was shirking his duties. Once in a while too, he was called upon to lecture at the Kitten Academy on his specialist subject, 'The True Value of Loyalty and Duty'.

For a long time, Horace stayed in his hiding place, looking down on the barn which had been his home for all that time of service to the brothers, and, slowly, it dawned on him that he was free of them at last – they didn't want him, and so that freed him to make a new life for himself, one of his own choosing and to his own liking, for whatever time he had left of his earthly life.

The distress and despair which had engulfed him at the realization he was not wanted, and that the brothers had tried to kill him, lifted from him, as if by magic, driven away now by the excitement he felt at the prospect of a new, and as yet unknown, life of adventure before him.

Horace would have been even more elated, had he known at the time, that in these twilight years of his life, he would not only find from one of his own kind the affection, love and loyalty he so richly deserved, but also would know the joy of starting a family of his own.

Horace sniffed the air, and then, setting his head high in expectation, he trotted off in the direction he fancied was beckoning to him to embark on his new life. His first priority he knew had to be to find food, but even the persistent pangs of hunger which beset him did not daunt his good cheer, as he set off, determined to make the most of the remainder of his earthly life.

Later that day, and entirely by chance, he would come across a place where he could eat his fill – a place he would one day describe to Grey Cat and White Cat as 'The Bothy'.

Curious Consequences

The day Lizzie plucked up the courage to investigate the curious object in the yard, which went away each day with the farmer's daughter, Mary, was to be the day Lizzie's life was to change for ever.

She left her bed early, with the idea of allowing herself plenty of time to get a good look at the object, before it left with Mary.

Hurrying across the yard on her stout little legs, she approached the object, and, with some trepidation, began walking around it, slowly, taking in every detail.

Some time went by before her courage allowed her to sniff at it. She didn't much like the smells of what she didn't know were petrol and oil, and she was none too keen either on the smell of the tyres.

The bright shiny handles on the doors, or, as she thought of them, wings, caught her eye and she jumped up as high as she could, to take a closer look.

After a number of abortive attempts, she had to accept she just couldn't reach them. It was as she landed heavily on the yard after her final attempt, that she noticed it – something brightly coloured hanging down underneath the object, swinging gently to and fro in the draught of air coming across the yard.

Immediately, she forgot the handles and was underneath the object, crouching on the yard beneath her feet, tapping the focus of her attention with her paw, and watching in fascination as it bobbed back and forth.

She was so engrossed with her new toy that she didn't see, or hear, Mary approaching. It was only when the object leapt into life with a loud roar that she realized she was in trouble. The object started to move off, and the tyres were so close to her that she had no time to flee and the only escape route from death available to her now, at that moment, was up.

Overhead, she could see a tangle of metal and wires, so she scrambled upwards, scrabbled about frantically to find a foothold, and clung on.

The object gathered speed and she was fearful for her life as she saw the ground racing by beneath her. The roar of the object was deafening. She closed her eyes, clung on for dear life, and prayed to the Lord Provider and Protector of Animals to deliver her from harm.

Her prayers were to be answered.

After what seemed like a lifetime to her, suddenly the object stopped, and, *so* suddenly, that Lizzie was dislodged from her perch, and fell heavily on the road, on to her back.

The fall knocked the breath out of her body, but she had the presence of mind to scramble to her feet quickly, and, before the object started to move again, she dashed out from between its wheels, across the lane, and into the ditch at the side.

Having reached safety, she peeped out, and saw that the object was on the move again, turning from the lane on to which she had fallen, on to a wider and busier road, where it joined lots of similar objects, which she supposed to be its friends.

Lizzie stayed in the safety of the ditch until the sun was high in the sky, and it wasn't until then she began to comprehend the realities of her predicament. She had no idea how far she had come from home, or in which direction, and no-one knew she was there.

Unknown to her, the farmer had noticed her playing around the car, and then had seen his daughter get into the car, and be about to drive away. He had been upstairs in the farmhouse at the time, and had banged on the window, and then opened it and shouted to his daughter to attract her attention, to warn her the kitten was there, but Mary couldn't hear him over the sound of the engine.

Later in the day, he and his daughter would retrace Mary's journey along the lane, searching for Lizzie, and, had she stayed in the ditch, she would have been found.

Lizzie considered her plight. If she stayed in the ditch, she was sure that eventually she would die from hunger, or exposure.

Fearful as the prospect was to a young kitten, who had never before ventured beyond the confines of the farmyard, she decided she had no option, but to try to find her own way back home.

She had no way of knowing in which direction her home lay, so she trusted to luck and chose one at random. Had she known it, she needed to go south, but, unfortunately, she chose west, and set off in that direction – a decision which would lead her into a whole new life.

Lizzie's curiosity was matched only by her determination and stamina, and she just kept going and going and going, until she was utterly exhausted and could go no further. Every muscle in her little body ached, and her tiny paws were red and sore, and, to her dismay, still there was no sign of her home.

She yearned to be back home, in the safety of their barn, along with her mother, brothers and sisters. Desperate despair overwhelmed her and she burst into tears.

Lonely, cold and hungry, she could go no further. It was nearly dark, and already the creatures of the night were out and about.

The loud hoot of an owl somewhere overhead startled her, and she shrank closer to the ground as the bushes beside her rustled with one of the nocturnals going about his or her business.

To add to her predicament, it was beginning to rain; a fine mist of droplets clinging to her coat from the steady drizzle which was preparing to soak the countryside.

Young and inexperienced as she was, instinctively she knew that if she didn't find shelter for the night, she would die.

In the gathering gloom, she looked about her, and it was then good fortune chose to smile on her, as she spied a big old hollow tree.

She forced her aching limbs into action, and, tiptoeing awkwardly and painfully on her sore feet, she crept into the safety offered by one of the old kings of the ancient wild wood, whose majesty once mantled Ireland from coast to coast in green.

Thankfully, she sank down on to the soft and dry earthen floor inside the base of the old tree's trunk, and there, committing herself to the care of their Lord Provider, she tried to sleep.

Somewhere above her, in the upper bole of the old tree, she heard two squirrels arguing and complaining about a trespasser in the ground floor of their home.

Given the circumstances, Lizzie slept surprisingly well, and the next morning, although very hungry, she set off again in much higher spirits and with a lighter heart.

After all the rain of the night before, it was a beautiful day, with the damp vegetation glistening in the sunlight.

Lizzie wrinkled her nose in pleasure, as the wonderful smell of damp earth wafted into her nostrils.

After resting the night, her limbs were less stiff and painful than they had been the night before, and, although the pads of her paws were still very sore, she found that the now softer ground underfoot helped, and the mud produced by the previous night's rain was soothing.

For the rest of the morning, she walked steadily, without stopping at all to rest.

The sun was high in the sky when she thought she should rest a while, and, just as she was about to sit down on a soft, mossy mound, a farmhouse and farm buildings suddenly came into view through a gap in a hedgerow.

Her heart leapt with excitement. She had made it. She was home.

Her joy quickly evaporated as she approached closer and saw that, although not too dissimilar in appearance, it was not her home farm.

Maybe though, she could find some help there.

She approached timidly, looking about her for signs of life, but saw none.

Then she saw it – food! It was just sitting there, in a row of dishes beside an old water pump on the opposite side of the farmyard, and just begging to be eaten.

Throwing caution and good manners to the wind, she raced across the yard, and, being so very hungry, shoved her face deep into the succulent feast spread out before her, and hurriedly gulped down large mouthfuls.

She had eaten almost all she needed, when something hit her at speed and she was bowled over and flung into the air. As she instinctively turned her body in mid-air, to be able to land back on her feet, she glimpsed a huge, all black tomcat, glaring malevolently in her direction.

She landed on her feet, and found herself looking up into the eyes of the tomcat. His bright green eyes were narrowed into slits and he hissed menacingly at her.

She was far too frightened to speak, or to move, and so she just stood there, trembling.

The tomcat moved in closer, pushing his face close to hers. Then came his voice – low and threatening – as he said slowly and deliberately, 'You. You leave my food alone, and get yourself off my property, *now*.'

She nodded, but couldn't move.

'Did you hear me?' he said, raising his voice an octave. 'Clear off, you're not wanted here.'

She saw his large gleaming white teeth and looked down to where he was flexing two front sets of razor sharp claws, readying them for action.

Lizzie's eyes opened wide in terror and she started to apologize, in a tremulous, squeaky voice she couldn't seem to control.

Just at that moment, a stern voice shouted across the yard in the direction of the tomcat. 'Jack, what on earth do you think you're doing? Leave that kitten alone this minute.' Immediately, the tomcat flashed an exaggerated smile at Lizzie, retracted his claws, and promptly retreated across the yard, to begin fussing and purring around the legs of the farmer.

'That's better, and so I should think. Threatening babies indeed.'

The tomcat continued his salutations.

'Now, that's enough, you're forgiven.' said the farmer, 'You go on now and find a comfortable place for the kitten.'

The tomcat returned to Lizzie.

'Well, it seems you are to stay with us, so, go and finish eating, and then I'll get one of the others to show you to where you can sleep.'

He didn't repeat the exaggerated smile he had produced for the farmer's benefit, but he was as good as his word, and so it was that Lizzie settled into a new home with a new family.

Later on, she was to discover that Jack was not nearly as fearsome as she had at first thought. Once she had become a member of his household, he was cordial and caring towards her.

One of the others explained to her that he saw his job as keeping them all safe from harm, by guarding and protecting the territory in which they lived. He took his duty very seriously, and, when she had turned up so suddenly, he had thought she belonged to another neighbouring colony of cats and had been sent on ahead to spy for them. Until the farmer had interceded, it hadn't even occurred to him that she might be just a little lost kitten in need of help.

Although not always as thoughtful and considerate as the farmer at her old farm home, this one was kind to them and saw to it that none of them ever went hungry, or without veterinary treatment if they were sick.

They had the freedom to go wherever they pleased on the farm, and the bed Lizzie was allocated in the hay loft, amidst an abundance of sweet smelling hay, proved to be a practical and comfortable home, where she was to be very happy indeed.

She missed her old home and her family, and, several miles away, her own family, and Mary and her father, missed and were sad for her for a long while. It would have been of great comfort to them all had it been possible for them to know she was safe and happy.

Early Days

Grey Cat and White Cat had been born in a snug nest prepared for them by their mother, Lizzie, in a corner of a hay loft.

Everywhere was the sweet smell of hay, and the convivial sounds of horses and cattle in conversation nearby, and hens clucking as they busied themselves pecking about on the yard outside. For them it was a peaceful world of gentle domesticity, which, once their tummies were full of their mother's sweet, warm milk, lulled them into peaceful sleep.

They slept a lot at first, rousing only to suckle their mother's milk, but as the days passed by quickly, and once they could see clearly – and get their limbs to do what they wanted them to do – they were keen to explore.

Life was wonderful!

Their mother had been very diligent about their upbringing, impressing upon the two young sisters the cat code of behaviour. She wanted to be proud of them she said, and to know they would never let her down when they made their own way in the world.

She reminded them continually that should they ever be invited indoors into a human's home, they must be especially careful how they behaved.

On no account must they take liberties, but indulge only in investigating their surroundings to the extent to which they were specifically invited to do so.

There was to be no scratching of furniture or furnishings, and absolutely no fouling indoors, except in circumstances where a litter tray had been provided for that specific purpose. Their mother warned them that more kittens and cats had found themselves homeless because of slips in these two essential aspects of behaviour, than almost any other cause.

She also cautioned them about humans' behaviour towards cats and kittens, saying that most humans, and the small-sized humans they called their children, were kind to animals, but occasionally humans brought cats or kittens into their homes only as toys to amuse their children and that was always bad for those cats and kittens. When the children tired of playing with their new 'toys', neither they, nor their parents, could be bothered to care for the cat or kitten, who was then neglected and felt very unhappy at being unwanted and unloved.

There were also some humans, and small-sized humans, who, for some reason no-one could understand, treated animals cruelly, and, in a very serious voice, she told the two young sisters – who were listening very intently and anxiously to every word – that once they went out into the world, if they were neglected or mistreated in any way by humans or their children, they *must* run away.

'When they have once been unkind to animals,' she warned, 'they usually do it again, so *never, never* give them a second chance. Be sure to remember what I say, because it could make the difference between life and death for you.'

Grey Cat and White Cat did not forget their mother's stern warning.

As the day dawned, Lizzie knew it was to be a day different from all those since the birth of her two pretty daughters. Instinctively she knew this was the day they would go off to their new home and they would be lost to her for ever. It was hard to accept, but she knew it had to be, and resigned herself to the inevitable.

'Now dears,' she said to the two sisters, 'as you embark on this new chapter in your lives, I entreat you to remember all I have taught you, and, above all, remember to keep true to yourselves, and to each other.'

Inwardly, she just hoped the girls' new family would be good to them.

She watched, and waited, for the family to arrive at the farm.

Late in the day, the family arrived in the yard, and as mother, father and two children came out of the car, Lizzie did not like what she saw.

The two children, a boy and a girl, were grossly overweight, with fat, florid faces, and they were arguing loudly with one another.

They stopped only when they spied the hens and their chicks scratching in the dust of the yard's surface, whereupon, immediately, they ran across the yard after them, shouting loudly, and, in the commotion which followed, very nearly stepped on one of the day-old chicks.

The chick had panicked and had tried to reach its mother for protection, but the children were in the way. Both children were waving their arms about wildly as they then tried to grab the little creature, and, in the confusion, the chick was running about around their feet, but, narrowly missing injury, managed to dodge between them and escape to re-join the anxious mother hen.

The children then lost interest and re-joined their parents. Lizzie didn't like the then pouting expression of the girl child because they had failed to catch the chick, or the loud voice and pushiness of the boy.

Almost immediately, their indulgent parents 'rewarded' them for their 'disappointment' and they then had their mouths stuffed full of chocolate and sweets.

They were ill-mannered and very badly behaved, and Lizzie was shocked to see that despite having their cheeks bulging out with all that they had packed into their mouths, they were still talking loudly, and so were spluttering bits of the confectionery around them.

Then they started arguing again and were demanding to see 'their' two kittens. All the while, their parents looked on, smiling indulgently at them.

'Why don't they stop them?' Lizzie wondered. She would never have allowed any kitten of hers to behave in such a fashion, and most certainly not in company. It was unthinkable. Lizzie was startled out of her reverie as the boy child amongst the group of humans suddenly appeared in the doorway of the hay barn, and the mother cat deftly side-stepped out of his reach, as he lunged towards her, arms outstretched in an attempt to grab her.

Then there was chaos, as the rest of the boy child's family, and the farmer, came in. Everyone was speaking at once. The boy child and his sister were shrieking with excitement and, amid the noise and confusion, the two kittens were being passed around from human to human, each one holding them up, stroking and tickling them.

The sisters were thrilled. To receive such attention from so many humans at once, they surely must be the most important cats in the world.

'Aren't we just the luckiest of cats,' cried White Cat, and Grey Cat had to agree. Then they were back down on the floor of the barn again, and Lizzie just had time to embrace her two pretty daughters and wish them good luck and happiness on the road of life, before a travel basket was produced, which she knew would carry away her kittens from her, for ever.

Her heart was heavy, but she stifled her emotions as both her beautiful little daughters clung to her for the last time, both chattering excitedly to her about all the adventures they anticipated lay ahead of them in their new home.

Lizzie knew she could not alter their destiny, and it was pointless to let her own misgivings spoil for them their excitement of their 'big day'.

Anyway, perhaps she was worrying about nothing, and the life into which they were entering now would live up to all the expectations of her excited little daughters. She hoped, with all her heart, that destiny had decreed it would be so.

Nevertheless, her anxiety for them remained, and, although she couldn't remember exactly why, she had the disturbing feeling that history was repeating itself and what she had just witnessed with the departure of her own two daughters was somehow reminiscent of something which had occurred in the past in the lives of members of her own family.

In fact, although she, and her mother, had been born on a farm, her grandmother and her Aunt Carmel (actually her gran-aunt) had been born into a comfortable, domestic home to a pampered pet cat. When it had come time for them, and their brothers and sisters, to leave home for new homes of their own, in their case a bad choice had been made for the two sisters, and they were not long in their new home before they were forced to run away from the cruelty and neglect they suffered there.

Lizzie ran out into the yard and watched as the car, carrying her two beloved small daughters away from her, was driven across the yard, out of the gate, and then it was gone.

As the sisters were borne away to their new life, trembling with excitement, had they known, they would have been concerned to see the strangely worried expression on their mother's face.

When they were gone, and Lizzie knew then she would never see them again, she walked slowly and dejectedly back across the yard and then slipped quietly into her bed amongst the sweet smelling hay piled high in the loft above the barn, where her two daughters, now lost to her, had been born. There she lay down, and, covering her eyes with her front paws, she wept as if her heart would break.

Festivities

The sisters' first day in their new home was one of non-stop activity and excitement.

In a pot in the main room of the bungalow stood a large green tree, decorated from top to bottom with bright shiny ornaments and draped all around with strings of sparkling tinsel. At its foot, were piled mysterious looking packages, all wrapped in pretty shiny paper.

The walls of the room were decorated with swags of red-berried holly and, through an archway, the girls could see a table laden with food.

The kittens were fascinated by the tree, and, when they clambered up the pot to tap the baubles on its branches, there were delighted shrieks from the boy child and his sister, while the adults looked on, smiling their amusement and approval.

Early in the day, brightly coloured ribbons had been tied into bows around the kittens' necks, which made them feel very important members of the family, but they were becoming quite overwhelmed now by all the attention they were receiving from the children, and from being picked up and fussed by every one of the many callers coming to the house.

The girls noticed that each visitor arrived carrying

brightly wrapped parcels, which were then added to the growing pile of similar packages beneath the tree.

Later in the day, all the packages were opened, and then there was all the brightly coloured wrapping paper strewn around the floor. The girls found the discarded crumpled paper totally irresistible and so there was loud

laughter then from the adults, and shrieks of excitement from the children, as the kittens played and rummaged amongst it.

To the sisters' surprise and delight, amongst the pile of packages had been two small ones – one for each of them.

The boy child had opened White Cat's for her, and the girl had opened Grey Cat's. Inside were tiny toy balls, with bells inside which jingled. Despite being very close to total exhaustion by then, the girls showed their appreciation for their gifts by chasing the balls around the room.

They were very young, and so very tired, and they longed for sleep, but the attention from everyone continued, and the children still expected them to play.

They struggled on, and, what had started out as a day of excitement and pleasure for them had rapidly deteriorated into an exhausting test of endurance.

It was not until the children, their parents, and several visiting adults went through the archway into the adjoining room, to sit at the table and start on the feast set out there, that the kittens had any respite from constant activity and were able to take advantage of the very welcome chance to creep away and hide out of sight behind a settee, to sleep.

They knew little of the rest of the day, staying fast asleep in their hiding place, and, fortunately for them, because by that time liberal amounts of alcohol had been consumed by the adults, and the children had become preoccupied with all their many other gifts, no-one missed them.

It was already dark outside when the kittens awoke. As they emerged from their hiding place, the girls saw that the children were asleep on the settee – and it was the children's parents who took the sisters back to their bed.

Growing Up

At their new home, Grey Cat and White Cat slept in a small shed outside, and every day the boy child and his sister would come to the shed, carrying a dish of delicious food for each of them and another of cool, fresh water to drink, and then they would remake the kittens' bed, to see that the bedding was clean and comfortable.

Then there was the fun of playing in the garden, chasing bits of string and tapping squeaky toys, to the delighted shrieks of the two children.

The kittens were cuddled a lot, and, heeding their mother's advice, they purred their appreciation for the love and attention lavished upon them.

The children also took them indoors and they, and their parents, noticed the kittens' impeccable manners. The sisters knew their mother would have been proud of them. Life was wonderful, and both sisters relaxed, believing they would be loved and wanted there for the rest of their lives.

Sometimes though, they found the children handled them rather too roughly, grabbing at them wildly and thoughtlessly without warning.

On one particular occasion, the girl child and the boy child were arguing about who would hold Grey Cat and the boy tried to pull her away from his sister.

Grey Cat tried not to make a fuss and cry out, but, as he tugged at her front legs, and the girl child clung fast to her back ones, it hurt so much she couldn't stop herself shrieking in pain.

At that moment, the children's mother came into the room and shouted at them both to behave themselves and to stop arguing.

The boy child, surprised and angry at the admonishment, thrust Grey Cat so violently towards his sister that she clung tightly to the child with her claws, whereupon the girl screamed, flung Grey Cat to the ground, and ran to her mother, crying, 'That horrible thing's scratched me.'

Her mother, exasperated by all the noise and arguments, sent her and her brother outside to play, and then grabbed Grey Cat and White Cat firmly by the scruffs of their necks. Then, dangling helplessly and uncomfortably, they were held at arm's length by the children's angry mother (who actually didn't like cats) and borne off down the garden path to their shed. There they were thrust roughly in through the open door and, once inside, the door was banged closed behind them.

They were in disgrace!

'I'm sorry,' said Grey Cat to White Cat tearfully, 'but I couldn't help crying out, the boy child was hurting my legs so badly, I thought they would break.'

White Cat ran to her sister's side. 'There, there, don't upset yourself. It wasn't your fault.'

Grey Cat nodded, glumly.

White Cat continued, 'I don't know why the children were being so rough and unkind. Had they been kittens, it would have been different. I'm sure that if we had behaved like that Mother would have punished us.'

They fell silent for a while, remembering their dear mother, who, although she had been strict in their upbringing, had been full of love for them, and always fair and kind. Both smiled as they thought fondly of their dear mother, whom they had had to leave behind when they left for their new home.

Party Time

It was on a sunny morning at the beginning of March that the sisters peeped from the small window of their shed and saw several of the same people who had been present at Christmas once again arriving at the front door of the bungalow, carrying gaily wrapped parcels.

The girls had grown considerably since the previous celebration on their first day at the bungalow, but were immediately excited at the prospect of another party and looked forward to wearing their ribbons again, although they did have some concern as to whether the bows would still fit them. Nevertheless, they groomed themselves extra carefully. They wanted to look their best in their bows, and perhaps there would be more presents for them too.

Then they waited for the children to come to collect them, to join in the festivities. All day they waited, and waited, and waited, and no-one came near their shed.

Nevertheless, they remained hopeful, and it was not until they saw the guests preparing to leave again, that they understood. They were not invited to the party and there were to be no bows, and no celebrations, for them.

The sisters' spirits sank.

They felt hurt, and humiliated, to realize they were not wanted there.

'Ah well,' said White Cat, trying to sound much more cheerful than she felt, 'perhaps we got it wrong and it wasn't a party after all...' Her voice trembled and trailed off, lamely.

'Yes, perhaps.' said Grey Cat, miserably.

'Anyway,' said White Cat, 'what do we want with parties, when we have each other... and that's all that really matters.'

Remembering the wisdom of their mother's words about remaining true to each other, Grey Cat said more cheerfully, 'Yes, you know you are quite right.'

Although they didn't fully appreciate it at the time, as the days and weeks wore on, the bond between them was to become ever more important, and ultimately would prove to be their lifeline to survive the rigours of what lay ahead of them in an ever more uncaring home.

Spurned

The sisters were nearly fully grown when they started to notice the really marked change in the two children towards them. It was undeniable, they were becoming less and less interested in their company.

There was no more play in the garden, and no more visits indoors. The girls were getting worried. They were desperate to get the children's attention. At every opportunity, they fussed around their legs, purring loudly, and tapped them with their paws, but, instead of being delighted as once they had been, now the children always seemed irritated by them, and roughly pushed them away.

White Cat and Grey Cat were bewildered; what had they done wrong?

The boy child was preoccupied now with the pleasures of his new bicycle, which he had been given on his birthday in March, and the girls could see through one of the windows of the bungalow that his sister was devoting more and more of her time to be in front of her mirror, experimenting with hairstyles and make-up.

Unbeknown to the cat sisters – shut away in their shed now for hours on end – life for them was to get worse.

It was late one morning, and, although they could not see out through the thick grime on the glass of their small window, the sisters knew it was a warm sunny day outside. What was wrong? Neither the boy child, nor his sister, had come with their breakfast. It was very hot and stuffy in the shed, and yesterday's food was beginning to smell, and, smelling even worse, was their fouled and wet litter tray.

They waited and waited, and still no-one came.

In the heat of the shed, Grey Cat drank daintily, wrinkling her nose in disgust at the taste of the stale tepid water.

What had happened? Had some awful accident befallen their two friends – the small-sized people who had loved and cared for them? The two sisters were very worried. The day wore on.

Dusk fell and the night began. Still there was no sound or sign of anyone, and the sisters settled down to sleep – and so began a restless night for both of them, of sleep tormented by dreams of their two friends meeting with a terrible fate. Unknown to them then, this was to be the first of many restless nights tormented by terror-filled dreams.

The next morning dawned, and it was even hotter, stuffier, and smellier in the shed. The two sisters were panic stricken at their imprisonment with no fresh water or food, or clean litter to use.

The day wore on and their desperation increased. It was now late afternoon and no-one had been near them for nearly two days.

Suddenly, there was a rush of cool air, as the door of their shed swung open, and there was the girl child with a dish in her hand.

She looked sulky and resentful. Nevertheless, the sisters ran forward to greet her, loudly purring their pleasure at the sight of their friend.

Surprised, they fell back as she put out her foot, pushed them roughly back into the shed, and, pausing only to push the dish towards them, slammed the door shut again. They looked at each other with sad, tear-filled eyes. What had they done wrong?

They didn't know, and couldn't begin to guess.

It was some time before they could bring themselves to eat the food in the dish, and it was then that they realized that the girl child, whom they had thought of as their friend, had neglected to bring fresh water and a clean litter tray.

They looked at each other in misery, and Grey Cat began to weep softly.

One evening, as they sat alone in their shed, beside their dishes of stale food and dirty water, with another night on their dishevelled and dirty bed facing them, White Cat said to Grey Cat, 'Do you remember Mother's warning about not staying where we are not loved and wanted?'

Grey Cat looked at her glumly, and, with a tear rolling down her cheek, said, 'Yes, I do, but why don't they love us any more?'

'I think,' said White Cat, 'they never really loved us at all. When we were small, we were just little fluffy toys to them and now we're bigger, they're bored with us.' She continued, 'Whatever we do, we will never be able to make them love us.'

Grey Cat nodded, 'Yes, you're right. It's just as Mother

said, we were just cute fluffy toys to them and now we're nearly grown up, they don't want us any more.'

They were silent for a moment, as they both felt the flutter of fear through their bodies. 'Well,' said White Cat at last, 'one thing's for certain, we can't stay here. We can't go on living in this smelly shed and eating rotten food. We're going to be ill eventually, and then what, no-one's going to do anything to get us well again.'

They both knew what they had to do.

The thought of leaving and going off into the unknown terrified Grey Cat, but, controlling the tremor in her voice, she said, 'Yes, I know. We will have to leave.'

The decision to leave presented the cats with a problem, as, nowadays, seldom were they allowed out of the shed. Whenever anyone from the house did come to the shed to shove a few scraps of food in through the door, they would be roughly pushed back, away from the doorway. How then were they going to be able to escape?

Freedom

One stormy night, as the wind howled around their shed, and the rain pounded on the roof, the girls huddled together on the corner of a dirty blanket and beseeched the Lord Provider and Giver of Life to deliver them from their peril.

Their prayers were to be answered.

They slept fitfully, with their shed shuddering, rattling and creaking before the force of the wind, and the rain dripping steadily in through a hole in the roof.

It was now well into Autumn, and this night their shed was even colder than usual, as the keen wind found its way under and between the wall planks.

When they awoke, something warm was caressing their flanks. Still half asleep, momentarily Grey Cat thought their mother had come to rescue them and she was gently caressing them, as she had done when they were born.

Then she was startled from her sleepiness by the cry of White Cat, who leapt up and shouted, 'It's sunshine,' and Grey Cat saw that indeed it was a shaft of golden sunlight which had held them in its embrace.

Together they looked to see from where the light was coming and saw a hole in the back of their shed. A short plank had been buffeted by the wind until it had rocked free from the nails which had held it in place.

The girls exchanged glances and then, with one last look around the shed which had become their prison, they scrambled through the gap. Then, with their breath coming in short gasps, and hearts thumping for fear of discovery, they knew they were free.

The sisters stood at the back of the shed for a few seconds, rejoicing in the warmth of the sun on their faces and their freedom, before hurrying off down the field before them. They could scarcely believe it – freedom!

After the fury of the storm the previous night, the world had transformed into a glorious sunny morning, with a light dew on the grass and the birds singing in exultation.

The girls set off at speed, to they knew not where, but anywhere had to be better than life in that stinking shed.

Partnerships

While, throughout the Winter months, Grey Cat and White Cat managed as well as they could as 'independents', by Spring more and more Grey Cat found herself looking out for Horace, and, after each chance meeting with him, was looking forward to being able to see him again.

Horace was kind, attentive, caring and courteous – all the qualities Grey Cat regarded to be of true value in a life partner. Although an older cat, he was very handsome still, and, whenever he looked at her, or spoke to her, she blushed and felt her heart flutter with excitement and pleasure.

Grey Cat didn't know it at the time, but in fact Horace was taking every opportunity to seek her out, because, from the very first moment they had met, he had adored her.

By late Spring, each knew they had met their life partner, and one warm early Summer evening, silhouetted in the rosy glow of the setting sun, Grey Cat and Horace stood beneath the local Trysting Tree and pledged their love, and their lives, each to the other, to the exclusion of all others.

White Cat also had met her life partner, but tragically, not too long after they had met in the moonlight, under the same Trysting Tree, and had made their vows to each other, poor dear honest Oscar was knocked down and killed by a passing vehicle, which did not stop.

And so it was that White Cat's kittens were destined to be fatherless on earth, and she would remain without a partner for the rest of her earthly life.

Horace was dying. He knew it, and Grey Cat knew it too, but she wouldn't admit it either to Horace, or to herself. All the time it was not acknowledged, perhaps death couldn't, or wouldn't, enter their lives and take him away from her.

'My darling,' said Horace to Grey Cat one evening as they sat together on the edge of their bed before retiring for the night. He paused, as his breath came in shorter and shorter gasps, 'now listen closely to me,' he stopped again to get his breath, 'should anything happen to me before our babies are born, promise me you will go on to The Bothy, where, without me, you and the little ones will be safer and will want for nothing.'

'Of course, of course, my dearest Horace,' said Grey Cat, 'I promise, but nothing is going to happen to you, and, just as soon as you are well again, we will be going on there together.'

Even as she spoke, she feared it would not be so, and Horace noticed the tears glistening in her eyes.

She coughed to cover what was threatening to be a sob and, in as a-matter-of-fact tone as she could muster, said, 'Now, Horace, no more of that sort of talk from you. It's getting late, and you need your rest to get well again.'

Then, snuggling down beside him, she kissed him goodnight and fell into a deep sleep from the exhaustion brought about by the anxiety she felt about his condition.

Horace sank back on to the bed, exhausted by the effort of speaking.

He lay awake throughout most of the night, watching his beloved Grey Cat as she slept softly beside him.

As he bent over her, gazing lovingly upon the love of his life, he told her silently how much he loved her and how his love for her would never die; he would love her until the end of time. He would be at her side always, until the time came for them to be together again, for ever. He told her of how she was the best thing ever to happen to him in an otherwise lonely life of drudgery, deprivation and devotion to duty, and of how he wished they could have had many more years together before he had been called to move on.

He continued to gaze down on her softly sleeping form and he wondered at this beautiful, enchanting young creature choosing to link her life with his, and of how much he adored her and their kittens soon to be born. Meeting Grey Cat, and starting a family with her, had made sense of all the rest of his dreary, monotonous life. She had made him the happiest, and luckiest, cat in the world.

He could move on now, happy in the knowledge that his life indeed had been well spent, because he knew now that, after all those years of suffering and waiting, he had at last fulfilled his destiny; he and Grey Cat always had been meant for each other. They had had but a short time together, but they had shared a love of such intensity and magnitude they had had more than most enjoyed in a whole lifetime together. He was content.

He knew for sure that his earthly life now was very

nearly at an end, and he wanted to spare Grey Cat the shock and distress of finding his still and lifeless body after he had left it to continue his journey.

At the thought of how he must leave her now, to begin his last journey of this life, the tears rolled slowly down his cheeks, and, fearing he would break down and his sobs would awaken her, panting with the effort, he struggled to his feet, and, looking down on his beloved Grey Cat for one last time, he kissed her on the cheek so softly that she did not stir.

He whispered, 'I will love you for ever, my darling, and I will be at your side, wherever you may be, until we meet again, my love,' and then, tears still rolling down his cheeks, he turned, and stole silently out into the night.

In his hideaway, his last thoughts were of his beloved Grey Cat and the joy he felt at the prospect of the birth of the family she was soon to bear him. He thanked their Lord Provider for the blessings of affection, love, loyalty and joy which Grey Cat had brought to him so late in his life. Then, much as he had lived, he passed quietly from the earth, alone, and with no fuss or bother.

Grey Cat awoke feeling rested and refreshed.

She had had such a wonderful dream – of her beloved Horace. He was as handsome as ever, but younger than when they had first met. He was happy and smiling, first drifting a little away from her, but with his paw outstretched to her, and then close by her again, gazing upon her, with his love for her shining in his eyes. He had whispered softly to her of his love for her, of how he would never leave her, and of how he would be with her wherever she went.

She turned to tell Horace of her wonderful dream of him, and, on seeing his empty place, she understood.

He had already left on his final journey and, although he would remain close by her, as he had promised, she would not be with him again until her time on earth was done too, and they would be together again then, for ever.

Dearest, thoughtful and kindly Horace, she thought, knowing he had chosen to slip away and die alone, rather than shock and distress her. He had spared her feelings, at the expense of his own.

The tears for him flowed down her cheeks, while she whispered softly to him of her undying love for him and for his babies who were soon to be born to her.

Silently she told the kittens stirring within her of how lucky they were to have such an exceptional, wonderful father, and of how he loved them too, so very much.

Part Two

The Barn Gang and the Pig House Crowd

Squinting their eyes against the sun's glare, Grey Cat and White Cat had followed the long wall and, at the big tree, turned to cross the grass field diagonally, from left to right. Then it was on across the plank (which was very wobbly and slippery) perched above the waterfall, while in trepidation as they crossed, they watched the water gurgling and chuckling below, on its way down the hillside.

As they stepped off the end of the plank at the other side – or rather, in White Cat's case, tumbled off, paws in the air, as it tipped up – they turned left again and followed the bank of the stream downhill, until it disappeared underground beneath a thick hedgerow.

Here the girls paused, and, paw to temple in thought, ran through again in their minds Horace's directions to 'The Bothy'.

Both chorused together, 'Right.' and then set off alongside the hedgerow.

The hedgerow seemed to go on and on towards the horizon and, with the sun now obscured completely by gathering rain clouds, they could no longer rely on the sun's help to plot their course.

As the cold drizzle began, they became wetter and wetter, and colder and colder, and eventually had to admit to themselves, and to each other, that they were hopelessly lost. Cold and miserable, with their high hopes of spending the night at The Bothy dashed, they crawled in underneath the dripping vegetation overhanging the ditch beside the hedgerow. There they sat down and wept, succumbing to bitter disappointment, fear of what would become of them, hunger and cold.

Grey Cat, who had always had a weak chest, began coughing quietly, her body shaking and trembling from the effort. Her sister, although blessed with much more robust health, shivered again, and tried not to think of food.

As they huddled together for warmth, each wondered if they had been foolish to set out, as they had, into the unknown in search of a better life.

What if they never found The Bothy?

White Cat began to wonder if The Bothy could be a figment of Horace's imagination, and did not actually exist.

Grey Cat knew better though, knowing for certain that her beloved Horace would never be untruthful to anyone, about anything.

White Cat's thoughts drifted on.

Could he have made it all up just to impress two very impressionable young girls?

She didn't know, and anyway it was too late now, it was done and there was no going back, so it was pointless to be thinking such thoughts.

If they were never to reach their golden goal, and the end of life was to come to them here, in this wet, cold and miserable place, then so be it, and at least the end would come to them as life had begun for them – together.

They smiled into each other's eyes, each reading the other's thought, and, brushing away their tears, they drifted off into sleep, coloured by confused dreams of soft warm beds and more food than they could eat.

When White Cat awoke, still cold, wet and hungry, the drizzle had stopped and, by the light of the moon‑ which penetrated the gloom as it peeped out briefly from behind the storm clouds as they sped their way across the night sky, she thought she glimpsed the shape of a building.

She shook Grey Cat awake.

Grey Cat was too cold and too sleepy to think or speak coherently, and instead just stumbled after her sister, who had already begun to lead the way through a gap in the hedgerow. As they hurried along its opposite side, their limbs cold and stiff, there it was again, definitely the shape of a building.

From somewhere overhead, a roosting bird whistled, 'I can see you and you can't see me,' and, deep in the hedgerow, a mouse sniggered at their plight.

'Not that we can blame them,' thought Grey Cat, 'our kind has never been particularly kindly disposed towards theirs,' and, in her misery, there and then vowed that if she survived this ordeal, and was rescued from this harsh wild world of want, in the future she would go out of her way to be more tolerant towards birds, mice and all other small creatures.

The invisible bird continued, 'Cat, cat, cat,
See me
If you can, can, can

Ha, ha
Can't, can't, can't
I can show
The way
You must go, go, go,
But oh
No, no, no
You are on
Your own
Yes your own, own, own.'

The girls' anxiety increased. Neither of them could face, or survive, another cold, wet Winter of hardship. The Bothy *had* to exist, and they *had* to find it, and quickly.

Then, just as if their thoughts had willed it to do so, just at that moment what they were seeking came clearly into view.

There it was, just as Horace had described it.

They ran headlong towards it, and, as they stood in the yard, as if by magic, the storm clouds dispersed and the soft light of the moon illuminated all around them.

They hugged one another tightly, each with tears of relief and joy on her face.

Tired, cold and wet, now as she felt the new life stirring within her, Grey Cat knew for sure that they had found sanctuary only just in time. She was certain she and her sister, and their babies about to be born, would be happy here.

Looking about her, instinct told her that, in the safety of the barn before her, she could make a comfortable home for her kittens to come, and be able to raise them in an environment free from cold, wet and hunger. There would be lots of room for her and her family, and, as they explored further, she saw that White Cat already had her eye on a neighbouring old school building, which, long ago, had been abandoned by its human owners.

There was a lot to do to prepare for the kittens, but thought Grey Cat sleepily now, and stifling a yawn, that could wait until morning.

She and White Cat decided to stay together for the first night in their new surroundings, and, as they settled down to sleep in the barn, Grey Cat said sleepily to her sister, 'Besides being without my dearest Horace of course, there's just one thing now which makes me sad... I wish Mother could know that we're safe and happy.'

'My sweet sister,' chided White Cat, 'we are her daughters and, in the way of all mothers the world over, she knows.'

And, far away, in a corner of a hay loft, a mother cat smiled contentedly in her sleep, as she lay dreaming of her two pretty daughters.

While they lay, waiting for sleep to take away the exhaustion and hardship of their journey, the two sisters began to make plans for the happy future they knew lay ahead of them, but what neither sister knew was that White Cat would later move in to the old animal house adjacent to Grey Cat's barn, and that they and their families would then become known locally as 'The Barn Gang' and 'The Pig House Crowd'.

The Bothy

Grey Cat's barn stood across a concreted yard from an old stone and thatch farmhouse (Abe's and Cara's home).

The barn was about 12 metres long and in the front wall towards one end was a stable door opening out on to the yard, and, at the other end, double doors, which led out into the second of two small fields.

Attached to the barn, at a right angle and facing the yard, was an old animal house, which also had a stable door opening out on to the yard.

High up and set at intervals around the thick stone walls of both buildings were unglazed slit windows, which both ventilated the buildings and let in the light.

At the end of the old animal house was a gate into the second field, and, on the side of the yard immediately opposite, were old iron gates to the lane outside.

The land behind the barn was at a higher level than that of the yard and, through a gap in wild fuchsia hedging, stone steps from the yard led up into that field – which was divided from its neighbour only by willow trees and thick bushes beside a shallow ditch.

A gate, hung from a stone pillar built into the back wall of the barn, led into the second field.

At first, the field to the rear of the barn was flat, but

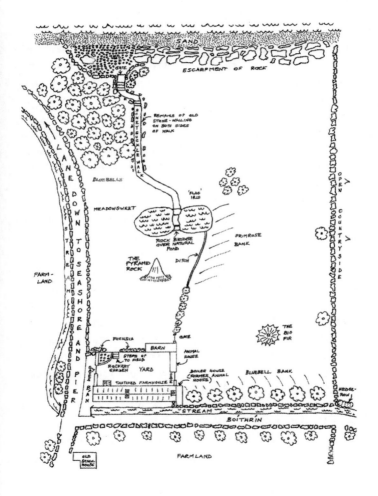

then began to slope downwards until, at its lowest point, it was divided from the remainder by a large pond, to one side of which was a boggy area with an extensive growth of fragrant meadowsweet, and, to the other, an expanse of wild yellow 'flag' irises. The iris end of the pond was overlooked by a grassy bank extending down from the higher level of the second field, and which, in Spring, was clothed in the delicate yellow of primroses in bloom.

The pond narrowed in the centre and it was there that access across it to the rest of the field was gained by way of a bridge of rock, comprising of three enormous boulders – one at each side, and a longer, flatter one than either of the others spanning the water between the two.

A path then led away from the pond uphill towards the headland, winding its way up through rough grass and bracken, to meet the beginning of an old path which was enclosed on both sides by the remains of old stone walling, over which tumbled a thick growth of wild woodbine.

To the left of the old path was a small copse of whitethorn and blackthorn trees, beyond which was another field, lying between the trees and the lane which had first passed by the front gates of The Bothy's yard, on its way down to the harbour and the pier, where local fishermen moored their boats and landed their catches of fish.

In the area to the right of the path, the bracken extended uphill until stopping abruptly at the edge of where the headland ended at an escarpment of rock which fell away steeply down to the seashore far below, where its boulders spilled out haphazardly over the pebbles and sand.

The second field at the homestead was comprised of

more pasture, and less bracken, but on its seaward side similarly ended abruptly at the steep rocky escarpment.

The only way down on to the seashore from either field was by way of the old path on the part of the headland which sloped away north-westwards.

At the end of the path, there descended a short flight of stone steps, followed by a corner turning to the left, and another longer flight of steps down to a small area shaded by a large whitethorn tree, and a gate.

Beyond the gate was the seashore.

Locally, the path was known variously as the honeysuckle, or woodbine, walk.

Family Cares

The next day, in the old school house, White Cat scarcely had time to find a suitable corner and gather together her birthing nest, before her kittens began to arrive.

The first of her young family to come into the world was Maxi, a robust black and white boy.

Next, in quick succession, were Pepper and Mori. Both the boy and the girl were of average size, healthy, and were silver tabbies almost identical in appearance.

The last to be born was Mary. White Cat saw that her own colouring had been replicated exactly in her younger daughter, but was very concerned to see that this kitten was very much smaller than any of the other three, and appeared rather frail.

It was of even greater concern to White Cat that, not long after her birth, Mary began to be troubled by a persistent cough.

In Pepper and Mori, White Cat could see something of her dearest Oscar. He had been true to the colouring of their wild cat ancestors with his brownish tabby coat and black paw pads, and, like them, he had not one hair of any other colour on his body. Although Pepper and Mori were lighter in colour than their father, she supposed her own predominantly white colouring would have been responsible for lightening theirs. She thought wistfully of Oscar. Such a wonderful, kind and affectionate character, whom she had loved dearly. He had been so jolly too, and, in the short time they had had together, their lives had been full of laughter. She smiled affectionately, as she remembered how, inclined as he had been to plumpness, whenever he laughed, his whole body shook with his mirth.

Then tears welled up in her eyes. It was so hard to accept that it had taken just one careless and uncaring driver, driving a vehicle too fast, to rob them of their happy life together, and to rob these enchanting babies of their father – the most affable and utterly adorable of cats.

She knew that to a driver like that one, it would have meant nothing at all to leave an anonymous cat dead at the roadside, never knowing, or caring, that his victim had a name and meant all the world to his little family.

Dabbing away her tears with her paws, she sighed, she knew there was nothing she could do to change what had happened to her darling Oscar, and all that was left of him to her now was to honour his memory, and the love they had shared, by raising his kittens to the very best of her ability. In them, and their descendants, dear Oscar would live on.

She turned her attention to the task in hand, smiling down on her brood, while she caressed each of them in turn with her tongue as she cleaned and dried them. Then, after they had been suckled, and were becoming drowsy, she settled down with them to sleep. It had been an exhausting morning.

Almost immediately after the birth of her kittens, White

Cat began to regret her choice of setting up home in the old school house, and, with the constant reminder of Mary's coughing, she blamed herself for her young daughter's continuing poor health. Never should she have chosen the old schoolhouse as a birthplace for her kittens.

Although the building was still more or less waterproof, the rooms and corridors were inclined to damp, and were draughty because several of the windows facing the sea were broken, and so, in addition to the problems of keeping her brood warm and dry, there was a lot of broken glass around, which was a hazard to growing kittens and made her job of keeping them safe from harm very much more difficult.

Why humans went to a lot of trouble and work to build snug and warm shelters, only to abandon them again to fall down, was beyond her.

One night when she had met her sister, she had discussed her problems with her, and Grey Cat had suggested she might be better off in the snug accommodation the old animal house next to her barn had to offer. If she moved in there, it also had the added advantage that she would not need to be running to and fro every night to collect food to take back for her kittens.

Not too long afterwards, on a day when the wind had skipped away with more of the tiles from the schoolhouse roof and had broken more of the windows, White Cat made the decision to move house.

She called her two daughters and two sons together, and explained to them the wisdom of moving into the alternative accommodation next to their aunt's home.

Mary, Maxi and Pepper immediately were happy and

quite excited at the prospect, but Mori, who had been born with a highly developed instinctive fear of humans, was horrified. She was so very frightened of what her mother was proposing for them all that her breath was coming in short, excited gasps.

Then came the words which, even as she was uttering them, she knew she would regret for the rest of her life.

'It's your fault Mary is so weak and ill.' Once she had started, she found she couldn't stop. 'You chose this awful draughty place for us – and now you want to risk our lives around humans.'

'I don't trust them, any of them,' she shrieked, and then, cheeks flushed with excitement, 'I tell you *I will not* go with you.'

White Cat was stunned at the ferocity and unjustness of her daughter's outburst. It was true Mary's delicate health was suffering because of the conditions in which they were living, but she had always tried the best she could to be a good mother to them, which was precisely why she was suggesting the move to a better place.

She stared at her daughter in disbelief and then quietly told her to go to bed. Afterwards, trembling and nauseous with the hurt and shock at what had been said to her by one of her beloved daughters, she crept into her bed and there, covering her face with her paws, she wept softly into the night.

The next morning, she and the others awoke to discover Mori was gone. She had left in the night, without a word to anyone.

Fergal, Aine, and Aoife

In the barn, Grey Cat had had troubles and tragedy of her own. Her four kittens were born safely the morning after she and White Cat had spent their first night at The Bothy, and it was very shortly after White Cat had left to set up home in the old schoolhouse, that they began to arrive, arriving quickly, one after the other, on the makeshift birthing bed she had hurriedly gathered together.

Felix came first. He was a large glossy black and white kitten and, to be honest, a bit of a disappointment for looks, with his less than handsome, wrinkled and screwed up face, and the seemingly shapeless lump of his body.

Grey Cat did not have the time though to dwell for long on the shortcomings in appearance of her first born, being almost immediately preoccupied with the birth of his sister. Aine was small and dainty. She was of the same colouring as Felix, but, thought Grey Cat, so very pretty, with her white bib and paws.

Aoife was next to arrive. Again the same colouring, and just as dainty and pretty as her sister.

Last was Fergal, and Grey Cat wept tears of joy when she saw he was the image of his father, her dearest Horace. In his snowy white coat, figured with glossy jet black patches, he was so, so handsome.

She turned to look at poor Felix, and wondered how two brothers could be so unalike, but, she reminded herself, in spite of his over-large ears and lop-sided expression, a good strong lad, with glossy black coat, white face, white paws and just the one white stocking. She saw that one white stocking as the only hint of herself in any of them. She failed to recognize that she had contributed the dainty, pretty features with which her two little daughters had been blessed.

Still, three good looking ones out of four was not bad, and the important thing was that at least Felix was healthy. Hopefully, his looks would improve, although, worryingly he appeared to have a speech impediment and she hoped that his stutter would not hinder or impair his development.

She knew it would be tempting to concentrate her attention on Felix's three siblings, who were as near perfect as possible in her eyes, but she must try not to show favouritism and deepen poor little Felix's sense of inferiority, which she feared might already be present. In fact Felix was blissfully unaware of his mother's disapproving opinion of his appearance as he snuggled up close to her and suckled her warm, sweet milk, with his handsome brother and pretty sisters all stationed alongside him.

As Grey Cat lay nursing her brood, how she wished dear Horace had been there, to share this moment of joy. She spoke to him silently, and then knew that indeed he *was* there with her, enjoying the moment too, and he was proud of their family.

For the next five days, Grey Cat stayed in the barn, in close and constant attendance upon her four kittens, every day thanking their Lord Provider for their safe delivery. At dusk on the sixth day, however, she surrendered to the primeval call of the night, which was urging her to go out and explore the nocturnal world. She knew too that she needed to keep fit, to be able to provide a plentiful supply of nutritious milk to feed her young ones.

All her kittens were fed, and were fast asleep, lying on their backs, with their full tummies protruding like little puddings from between their short, stubby legs.

They're fine, she reassured herself, and I'll keep close by. Anyway, I won't be gone long. After being confined indoors, as she stepped out into the night, she breathed deeply of the cool night air. Wonderful, she thought.

True to her word, it was not long before she was on her way back to the barn, and, as she approached the slit window she had used to leave the building, she fancied she glimpsed a shadowy shape, but, in the gloom of that moonless night, she couldn't make out what it was. Despite her keen eye-sight, she could see virtually nothing, but what she did notice though, was a whiff of a foul, offensive odour in her nostrils as something passed her and made off into the night.

She jumped up easily, and in through the slit window. Immediately she went to check on her babies and she felt a glow of pride and love as the piping voices of her brood greeted her – 'Mamma', 'Mamma', 'Mamma'.

Just a minute, though, there was something wrong. Something didn't look right.

One, two, three, she counted. She counted them again. One, two, three, and then, to her horror, she realized little Aine was missing.

Frantically, she searched the barn from end to end, but there was no sign of her little daughter.

There was no way any of her small babies could have reached any of the slit windows to get out of the barn, and she knew then that Aine had been abducted.

She knew too that she had no hope of finding her.

She settled down with the others to nurse them, as, by now, they were long overdue for a feed, and, as they gurgled contentedly at her breast, she tried to stifle her sobs for her little lost daughter.

She had tried to question them about Aine's disappearance, but they were so little, they could tell her nothing intelligible. She knew she had to accept that Aine was gone.

Grey Cat mourned her lost daughter, and tried to force her self to remain in the barn at all times, but that primeval call to her kind was just too strong to be resisted and, as the light faded again, she felt compelled to go out into the night.

Next to disappear was her beloved, handsome Fergal. She wept desperate, bitter tears for him. She had seen nothing of his abductor, but noticed that same unpleasant smell lingering in the barn.

When Aoife was gone too, she thought her heart would break.

She was left now with only big, clumsy Felix for company, and she believed she was being punished for her foolish pride in the good looks of her handsome son and pretty daughters, which had been at the expense of poor, ungainly Felix.

She knew her disappointment in Felix had been unkind and unfair to him. He was as their Lord Provider had sent him, and she should have shown him the love he deserved. She resolved there and then to start making it up to him right away, and, provided he survived the night predations of the unknown being which had taken her other three kittens from her, from now on she would devote her life to Felix's upbringing, education, and well-being.

Grey Cat had tried to question Felix about the disappearance of his brother and sisters, but he couldn't tell of how first he had heard the shriek of Aine, as she was carried away, next his brother, Fergal, struggling and screaming, and finally his little sister, Aoife, whimpering and pleading with the monster to let her go. He couldn't tell her either of how he had then lain there, trembling, waiting for his turn to come when the monster returned again for him, as he had been certain it would. Why his turn never came, he didn't know.

He had never seen what form of monster it was which was terrorizing them, but he had felt its hot, rather smelly breath as it leaned over, waking the sleeping infants. When it arrived, the terrified kittens had lain absolutely still, desperate for their mother's protection, but the monster was crafty and always came when their mother had had to leave them for a short time, and it was gone again before she returned. When Aine and Fergal were gone, then there was that last awful night, when, as he and his little sister, Aoife, snuggled up together, there was the hot, smelly breath again, and then cool air on his back in place of the warm body of his sister. He had stretched out his little legs in this direction and that and discovered, to his horror, that he was alone. Trembling and cold, he had lain there, expecting to be snatched from his bed at any minute, but instead, he had heard the welcome sound of his mother returning.

When Grey Cat had asked him what had happened, he was too young, and too terrified, to speak coherently, and instead had spluttered, stuttered, and burst into tears. She had comforted him as best she could, but he was inconsolable. He and his brother and sisters had talked about how they would run and play together as soon as they were old enough to do so, and now that would never happen – he was on his own now, and he could only guess, and shudder, at the others' fate.

Grey Cat was distressed for Aine, Fergal and Aoife, and concerned about Felix. Cara was concerned for them all. Only Felix knew what had happened, and he was too young to be able to tell.

Felix had wanted to tell Cara that his brother and sisters had been abducted by a monster in the night, but, as even his own mother couldn't understand his infant gabbling, he knew he had no hope of getting a silly human to listen to him.

Grey Cat resigned herself to the fact that she would never know what had happened. Felix was too young to be able to tell her, and, by the time he was old enough to do so, the detail would already have faded from his conscious mind, and, anyway, by then she would be beginning to forget exactly what it was she wanted to ask him.

In his wisdom, their Lord Provider, who watched over all animals, had blessed them with the inability to continue to grieve over events they could not change. Humans hadn't been so lucky. But then, she thought, maybe they didn't deserve to be. Their sins against the animal kingdom were legion.

She knew that, without the regular renewal of their bond by being in each other's company, it would not be too long before her beloved Horace would be fading from her too.

She sighed.

Ah well, that was the way of things and it was not for a little cat like her to question what was written for cats in the Book of Destiny, but she resolved, nevertheless, to remember him for just as long as she could.

In fact, it was Horace who came to her.

Recognition of an earthly life of hardship and deprivation so bravely endured, and his thanks, in his last moments, to his Lord Provider for the blessings Grey Cat had brought to him, had earned Horace the privilege of his love for her transgressing death and being able to watch closely over Grey Cat and Felix from beyond the grave. He could maintain contact with Grey Cat, to keep their love for each other alive.

They met up again in Grey Cat's dreams, and, one night, to her astonishment, standing beside him were her three poor lost infants, smiling up at him.

'Don't distress yourself so, my darling,' said Horace to Grey Cat, 'you mustn't blame yourself. You did your best, but the fact is that all our babies were not destined for your world.'

Grey Cat felt the tears of relief and joy flooding down her cheeks. She was too choked with emotion to speak, and Horace went on, 'They are safe and happy here with me, and I will care for them, as I know you will care for Felix. It's so wonderful for me to have them here with me, until the time we can all be together again. Be happy, my darling, and be sure to tell Felix that he has a father who loves him too.'

Through tears of joy, Grey Cat smiled at her beloved Horace and their three babies, and, as she kissed each one of them on the cheek, they began to fade from her.

She awoke, feeling rested and much more cheerful, knowing that her lost little ones were in the best of care and that her duty lay now to rear Felix to the best of her ability – and she was to set about the task with a vigour which Felix did not always appreciate was for his own good!

Felix

Felix, the first born, the largest, and the sole survivor of the Barn Gang family of kittens, was lying in his soft bed, and, at just ten days old, his eyes were beginning to open and he was surveying the world around him for the first time.

He saw his gentle mother, who was prettier than he had imagined, and he purred softly to himself at the thought of her warm, sweet milk which he suckled so greedily.

He saw that she was slim and dainty, with a sleek grey tabby coat, complemented by snowy white chin, chest, underside, front paws and hind stockings. Even with the rigours imposed upon her by motherhood, she was immaculate. He purred again, contentedly – surely his mother must be the most beautiful of all cats.

Grey Cat looked down on her son, with his lop-sided gaze, and laughed affectionately.

'You look like Long Cat Silver,' she said.

Felix felt silly, and his chubby cheeks flushed hotly under his fluffy baby coat, and, as his mother saw his little chin begin to tremble, and his one open eye begin to fill with tears, immediately she regretted teasing him.

'Don't worry,' she reassured him softly, 'it usually happens like that, and it won't be long before your other eye will open and you'll be able to see everything all around you properly.'

Felix was comforted, and settled deeper down into his soft bed, under the peculiarly soothing rasp of his mother's rough tongue on his one closed eyelid.

'Who is Long C-Cat Silver?' he asked, sleepily.

'Never mind that now, dear,' and his mother made a mental note not to forget to tell him the adventure story of 'Kitten Island', which had so enthralled generations of boy kittens.

Felix's mother studied her now sleeping son.

What a fine strong kitten he was, and so good natured – just like his dear father.

She so missed Horace, and thought wistfully of their happy union.

When they had first met, she had known he was a lot older than she, and had known for some time too that he was not a well cat. She had noticed how stiff were his limbs when he stretched each morning on rising from his bed – and then there was his cough, sometimes wracking his body so violently that he slid to the ground, gasping to regain his breath.

Oh how she wished he were here now, with his calm common sense, which during her pregnancy had assured her all would be well all the while she and the little ones had his protection.

Since he had stolen away to die that sorrowful night nearly two weeks ago, she had known, in the way only cats can know, that he would not return.

A tear for him slid down her cheek, and then came the

tears for her lost little ones too. She had known how vulnerable she and her babies were without Horace to protect them, and (she shuddered at the thought), she suspected a new suitor who had tried to waylay her more than once, might have more to answer for than pestering her with his unwelcome attentions.

Waiting For Friendship

Once Felix's eyes were open, in common with all kittens of his age, he was keen to be exploring his surroundings, in search of adventure, and playing the days away.

Unfortunately for Felix, the loss of his brother and sisters meant he had no playmates, and, in the time before his aunt brought his cousins to live next door, he was a very lonely little kitten indeed.

His mother's heart ached to see him. He was such a sad little figure, the essence of dejection and humility, as he quietly went about the barn, or around outside in the yard, trying to find 'a game for one' he could play.

Grey Cat did her best to keep him entertained and occupied, but what he wanted, and needed, was company of his own age. Usually it was not long before all her efforts failed, when he would thank her politely and then creep quietly back into his bed again, pretending to be tired.

There he would stay, for hours on end, quietly longing for a playmate to come into his life.

It was there too that every night he prayed silently and earnestly to their Lord Provider to send him a companion with whom to share his kittenhood.

The arrival of his cousins was to be the answer to his prayers – and one of the happiest days of his young life.

Into the Wilderness

Baby Felix was missing! Grey Cat had left him playing in the barn that morning while she went off briefly to do an errand and, on her return, he was nowhere to be seen.

Having told him he was to stay in and around the barn during her short absence, when she couldn't find him, she was frantic with worry. After what had happened to Fergal, Aine and Aoife, she feared the worst, in thinking that he too may have been abducted. She searched both the barn and the yard again and again, in the hope that he was just playing hide-and-seek, but still there was no sign of him.

Starting with the two fields adjacent to the barn, she continued searching, calling his name all the while; her voice becoming shriller and shriller as time went on and she was having more and more difficulty controlling the rising panic of fear gripping her heart that she would never see her young son again.

She searched the ditches around the fields and then peered into every nook and cranny of the old stone walls beside them. He was so small, he could be anywhere.

Satisfied that he was nowhere in either field, she set off into the open countryside in search of him.

Unknown to his mother, the very first time he had

inadvertently ventured beyond the barn and the yard on his own, Felix had quickly run into trouble getting back home.

After his mother had left him late that morning, he was playing in the yard, when he was startled by the sudden appearance of a very large, brightly coloured bird (he would later come to know to be a cock pheasant), who skimmed in over the yard gates and then dashed across the yard, running and fluttering his wings at the same time. The bird pushed past him, nearly knocking him down, and then called back over his shoulder, 'Sorry. Can't stop. I've gotta go. Gotta hide.'

With that, the bird was across the yard and on across the small field beyond. Felix was alarmed, but also intrigued.

What *was* going on?

Hoping to find out, and, in his excitement for adventure, temporarily forgetting his mother's instructions to him to stay close to the barn, he hurried along behind the bird and, just as he had reached the field's old stone boundary wall, and had scrambled up and over the top of it to try to catch up with the bird, there was a very loud bang close by. Immediately, the bird took to the air, flying fast and low to the ground, until taking refuge beneath a thick hedgerow in the distance.

The gunshot so startled Felix, he lost his footing on the countryside face of the old wall and fell down heavily into the thick vegetation at the foot of it.

The fall winded him, and he was shaking with fear – fear of the gunshot, and then the fear of his mother finding out that he had disobeyed her instructions to him to stay within the confines of the barn and the yard.

Although he was still very scared of the gunshot, the thought of his mother's disapproval scared him more, so he decided he had best get back up the wall and back into the yard as quickly as possible, before she returned home.

It took him some time to disentangle himself from the undergrowth, which consisted mainly of long trailing briars which insisted on entwining themselves around his body.

Just as soon as he had broken free from one, another would take its place. It was not until he was free that he looked up at the wall and then saw, to his horror, that as the land dropped sharply away downhill from it, this side of the wall was twice or three times the height of the side facing the field at his home.

He knew he couldn't climb it and, with this formidable barrier between him and his home, the more he looked at it, the more he began to panic. He sat back down on the ground, whimpering in distress and fright, and it was a while before he calmed down sufficiently to consider his predicament rationally.

Eventually, he arrived at the logic that if he couldn't get over the wall to get back (which he knew he couldn't), he would have to explore, to find a way around it to get home.

He knew that he would be in trouble with his mother, because there was no way now he could get home before she returned, but the thought of not deliberately disobeying her now by exploring – because of being *forced* to do so – made the idea much more appealing to him.

He set off briskly, at first following the wall in one direction to see if the height of it reduced anywhere along its length.

At the point where the wall ended at the top of the headland, there was one really scary moment. He decided to peer over the edge of the cliff, to see if he could clamber around the end of the wall, and the discovery of the dizzy height of the headland above the seashore he could see so very far below him sent him scurrying back to the safety of the base of the wall.

He sat for a moment to catch his breath.

Then, having established that the wall in that direction was more or less uniform in height for its whole distance, and there was no way over, or around it, he doubled back to find another route.

As he approached the other end of the wall, he saw there was an old hedgerow extending outwards at an angle from that corner of the field. He pushed his way through at the bottom of it, to see if the wall of the field might be lower after it turned the corner.

He saw though that the wall extending away from that corner was even worse, in that not only was it higher still, but there was a fast flowing stream running along at the foot of it, and it was full to overflowing.

He couldn't cross the stream and, even if he could, he couldn't scale the wall. He turned back through the hedge and, with no other option, decided to follow the hedgerow.

At intervals he looked through the hedgerow to see if he could cross the stream and make his way back towards his home in a round about fashion, and he had walked for some considerable time and distance before he found where the bed of the stream obligingly disappeared underground, and there would allow him to cross.

Once through the hedgerow, he spent a few enjoyable minutes watching the water bubbling and gurgling its way up from underground to continue its journey down to where it skirted the extra high wall beside the field next to his home, and then he looked around him.

As far as he could see in every direction, there was open countryside, occasionally broken by clumps of bushes, a hedgerow, or a few trees.

It had taken him so long to come this far, the sun was already beginning to set and he knew it would not be long before nightfall, and then he would be alone, in the dark. He trembled with fear at the thought. He pushed that unpleasant prospect to the back of his mind, and decided that now he was over on the other side of the stream, he would follow the hedgerow in the reverse direction, back towards his home, in the hope that at some point beyond where he could see when he first saw the stream, there would be a way back into the field by his home.

He trudged along on his little fat legs until it was dark, and he was utterly exhausted. He knew it was dangerous for him to be wandering around in the dark on his own. Anyway, he could no longer see where he was going, and he was just too tired to take another step.

By chance, just as he had decided he would have to stop for the night, he saw he was by a group of thick furze bushes.

Shelter!

Crouching low to the ground, very carefully he pushed his way inside the circle of bushes and there, on the dry ground beneath them, he lay down, and, gazing up at the bower of sharp prickles overhead, he fell into a deep, exhausted sleep.

Felix awoke to the sound of birdsong close by. In the gloom of his hideaway in the thick bushes, he wouldn't have known a new day had dawned, but he did know that birdsong heralded the break of day.

He crawled out from his hiding place into sunlight, and was surprised to see that it had rained overnight.

Everything around him had been soaked by the overnight rain, and, seeing how very wet was the countryside around him, he thought himself very fortunate that the rain had failed to penetrate the thick roof of his overnight refuge. He must remember furze for the future, he thought, for those times when he might be in need of shelter from the rain.

For a while, he admired the beauty of the golden dome under which he had spent the night, its bright yellow blooms glistening with raindrops, and watched in fascination the ease with which brightly coloured snails glided along the branches of the bushes amongst the sharp prickles.

He looked around again, and noticed something he had missed in the gathering gloom of dusk the day before. It was a gate, beyond which there was a muddy *boíthrín*, deeply rutted with tractor tracks.

He made for the gate. When he reached it, he saw it was too high for him to climb, but the bottom bar was high enough above the ground for him to be able to squeeze under it.

Once through, he saw the way ahead stretched away into the distance, beside the stream, which, after the previous night's rain, was running still faster and beginning to spill over on to the *boíthrín,* already filling the ruts with water.

He tiptoed through the surface water onto the other side, away from the edge of the stream.

On this side, there was a sod and stone bank, with a thick growth of ferns and wild flowers, topped by a row of blackthorn bushes.

He continued on his way, and, after he had gone some considerable distance, he came to the remains of an old gateway, and, on his right, the start of the very high old stone wall he had seen the day before. Up closer, it looked truly enormous.

He walked on, stopping only to admire the glossy, fleshy pads of the navelwort hugging the wall and the beauty of the bloody-cranesbill, whose delicate fronds draped down the wall from where the plants were rooted in crevices between the stones.

He was utterly astonished by what then came into view.

He couldn't believe his eyes when he saw that the very high old stone wall gave way suddenly to what he recognized as a whitewashed wall of the old farmhouse at his home! He had made it. He had found his way home.

He trotted on and saw that where the *bán* of the old farmhouse met the lane beside the yard, the stream disappeared underground again. He turned sharp right on to the *bán* and then was scrambling under the pair of old iron gates back into the yard.

The yard was deserted. He called, 'Mamma' a few times, but she did not appear.

The barn door was closed, and he knew he couldn't reach the slit windows to get in, so he settled down to wait on the rockery garden by the gates.

The sun was high in the sky by the time his mother returned home. She had been relentlessly searching the countryside for him since the day before, and, when Felix saw her, she was walking slowly and dejectedly across the yard.

She was exhausted, and was despairing of ever seeing her young son again.

He called, 'Mamma, I-I'm here,' and, thinking of how very cross she would be with him, in some trepidation he rose to greet her.

To his astonishment, instead of scolding him, his mother ran to him, swept him off his feet, and clasped him tightly to her.

She rocked him to and fro in her arms, whispering over and over again to him, 'There, there, my poor, poor boy.'

He didn't understand why she wasn't cross with him for his disobedience, but, after the rigours of his unexpected, but not altogether unwelcome adventure, he was very glad that it seemed he wasn't going to be punished after all.

As his mother carried him across the yard and into the barn, he purred his gratitude for her understanding.

It was not until she had him safely back indoors that his mother began to question him about what had happened to him. He explained as best he could about the pheasant and the gunshot, and then, eyes filling with tears, he hung his head and told her how very sorry he was for disobeying her.

She smiled at him fondly, and, softly stroking his brow, said gently, 'Never mind about that now dear, all that matters is that you are home and safe.'

It was true, he was safe!

Felix asked his mother why the big bird would have been frightened and running away, and what was the loud bang he had heard?

Grey Cat explained slowly and carefully to her young son how some humans had dangerous things called guns, and took pleasure in shooting at big birds like the pheasant he had seen, and, if ever he heard a bang like that one again, he was to hide out of sight until the danger had passed.

She told him she couldn't understand why any of those humans would be shooting at pheasants at that time of the year, because that was not usual, and the pheasant Felix had seen must have been exceptionally unlucky to have come across one who would do so.

Immediately, Felix was concerned for the pheasant's welfare, but his mother told him not to trouble his head about things little cats couldn't change, telling him again that what mattered to her was that *he* was home and safe.

He smiled at his mother. He was delighted to know that he meant so much to her, but he hoped that the beautiful pheasant had found safety too.

That night, tucked up in his bed, he prayed to their Lord Provider, asking for the pheasant's safe deliverance from harm. He was never to know that his prayer had been answered.

A Close Shave

Like all lonely youngsters before him, to compensate for the lack of companions of his own age, Felix invented an exciting imaginary world of adventure of his own, and spent a lot of time in his imaginary world, where he was the fearless central character and hero.

It was during one of these flights of fancy that he very nearly came to very serious harm.

At last, he had found an exhilarating 'game for one' he could play: It involved the strange creature which shared his home in the barn. It was red and black in colour, with two black pouches at its rear end and a long black pipe above its mouth.

For most of the time, this mechanical monster rested quietly in a corner of the old barn, where, without protest, it allowed him to sit on its saddle and crawl under and over it. Felix took full advantage of its compliance.

Felix noticed that, from time to time, suddenly it would awake with a throaty roar, and then go outside with Abe from the farmhouse to eat the grass, roaring all the while. Sometimes, it was extra hungry and would go off up the road to eat more grass.

It was a very odd creature. It never answered him when he spoke to it, and certainly it had the oddest eating habits.

When it went out to eat grass, it ate lots and lots of it all in one go, and then it would come back into the barn and didn't eat again for ages.

Always on wet days it fasted, but it didn't seem to mind, just resting quietly in its corner. Felix, who had a very healthy appetite, tried to imagine what it must be like to eat only occasionally and to go without food for most of the time, and his tummy rumbled in protest at the thought!

One afternoon, he discovered that if he stood on tiptoe on the top of the mouth of the grass eating monster, he could just reach the long dark tunnel above it.

After a number of abortive attempts, eventually he managed to heave his small podgy body into the entrance to the tunnel.

Scrambling then uphill on a slippery surface wasn't easy, but Felix wedged his little fat bottom sideways in the tunnel and edged his way upwards.

At the top, he saw that the tunnel turned and then dropped down steeply into who knew where? He thought about climbing down it, but, as he couldn't see to where it went, or what may lay at the end of it, he decided to stick with the long tunnel he had climbed, so he turned, stuck out his little feet, and pushed himself off from the sides.

Down he slid, swaying from side to side, until he landed with a bump back on to the top of the monster's mouth.

Once he had discovered the joys of whizzing down the tunnel – 'The Great Slide' as he called it – there was no stopping him, and, until the arrival of his cousins to live next door, it became Felix's favourite game.

The more he used the slide, however, the greater his

curiosity grew about the other bit of the tunnel, which dropped away into the unknown. He would sit at the top of the slide for many cat hours, gazing down into its dark, hidden depths, trying to see what secrets it might hold.

Felix didn't understand, of course, the dangers of playing around machinery, and one fateful day, when, as he so often did, he was sitting at the top of the slide, peering down into the mysterious depths of the tunnel beyond, with his imagination busy turning it into an underground tunnel to caves full of pirates' hidden treasure, suddenly the monster roared into life.

The noise startled and completely deafened him, and, it was as he was trying to put his front paws over his ears to shut out some of the din, that the monster lurched into motion. The sudden movement dislodged him from his perch at the top of the slide, and he toppled head first into the tunnel before him.

Down he went in the dark, bouncing from side to side, until he landed heavily on to the floor of what appeared to him to be a cage.

The fall knocked all of the breath out of his body, and it was when he had got his breath back, that fear took over as he looked around him.

The roar of the monster's voice was unbearable and, as he then frantically ran around the cage, searching for a way out, he realized there was none, and he knew he was trapped. The monster must have eaten him!

His head was spinning from the noise, and the monster's lurching movements were making it impossible for him to keep on his feet.

In abject terror, Felix screamed and screamed at the top of his voice.

Then he thought he heard someone shout from somewhere nearby, and the monster's voice quietened.

By now, Felix was so dizzy, he was flat on his back on the floor of the cage, feeling really sick and ill. He lay there, panting.

Suddenly, the roof above him opened, and there was sunlight shining down into his prison, and then there was Abe's companion, Cara, looking down on him and talking to him.

She reached down towards him and he went to get up, but fell over again. Everything about him seemed to be whirling around, so he closed his eyes and waited for Cara to pick him up.

Once he was in her arms, he clung to her tightly, whimpering.

She was talking to him as she held him, but he could hear little above the roaring still going on in his head.

As he began to calm down, he heard Cara say something to Abe about it being very lucky he had not switched on the blades.

Cara set him down on the yard outside his home in the barn, but he was still so dizzy he couldn't stand up, and, every time she tried to set him on his feet, he rolled over again on to his back.

So, she sat him on her knee instead, and stayed with him for a long while, and it was not until he could balance again, and remain on his feet, that she left him.

He made his way into the barn slowly, hoping that his

mother wouldn't find out about his escapade. Fortunately, she didn't notice anything wrong, so he crept away into his bed, where, after all the excitement, he quickly fell asleep.

When he awoke from his nap, he felt refreshed. He saw the monster was back in its usual place in the corner. It didn't look angry at all. It looked just the same as always.

He thought for a minute about what had happened to him, and then made his way over to the monster. Well, after all, he had used 'The Great Slide' many, many times before, and it *was* just the once the creature had roared at him. It was probably just some silly misunderstanding!

Neighbours

One morning early, as Felix lay in his bed, day-dreaming about all the games he could play once their Lord Provider answered his prayers and sent him some companions of his own age, his mother's voice interrupted his thoughts.

'Get up, Felix, we've a busy day ahead – your aunt and cousins are coming to stay,' adding that they would be living in the old animal house next door.

Felix's mother was excited at the prospect of having her sister and her family close by. Over the time since they had arrived in their new homes, Grey Cat had seen her sister only when their paths had crossed on their nightly excursions, and neither had seen the other's kittens, so, when her sister had said she would have to move from the derelict schoolhouse where her family had been born, Grey Cat had suggested the old pighouse, and now today was the big day, when they would be moving in.

Obediently, Felix immediately rose from his bed. He didn't know he had an aunt and cousins. What were an aunt and cousins?

His mother was in a fluster and was busying herself so frantically about the barn, tidying this, tidying that, moving this to one place, and then, a few minutes later moving it back again, Felix knew it was not a good time to be asking her any questions, and so, for the remainder of the morning, he just did as he was told, when he was told to do it. At last everything was ready, to his mother's satisfaction, and it was as she looked about her, smiling with satisfaction at her, and her son's efforts, that the door opened, and Felix met his aunt for the first time.

He noticed that his aunt was plumper than his own mother, and she looked very matronly. She had a pure white coat, figured with pretty grey tabby patches, and he saw her tail was ringed with black and grey tabby stripes, identical to the colouring of his mother's tail.

His mother and aunt embraced, and then turned around to face him.

His aunt's exceptionally large greenish-brown eyes regarded him steadily. 'So this is your Felix,' said his aunt to his mother, 'What a fine boy.'

Felix was embarrassed at the attention, and so dropped his eyes and studied his own feet intently.

His mother and aunt then swept on by him, and he trailed after them into the yard.

There, standing in a group, were three youngsters.

His boy cousins were introduced to him first. He saw that Maxi was black and white, like himself, but with the eye-catching distinguishing feature of a black roundel on the white of his chest beneath his chin. Pepper was a handsome silver tabby. Both were friendly and looked as if they would be good sports, and fun to have around.

Last to be introduced was his girl cousin, little Mary, who, in colouring, was a miniature version of her mother.

Immediately he was attracted to her.

His mother was beautiful, but this tiny creature was, was… exquisite.

His heart missed a beat as she fluttered her long eyelashes, lowered her eyes demurely, and whispered huskily, 'Hello, Felix.'

Felix tingled all over and thought he would faint.

By the time he had composed himself, the vision of loveliness had glided on, and Felix glimpsed her slim and elegant figure disappearing into the old animal house behind her mother.

From that instant, Felix was in love.

Diplomatic Relations

From the beginning, the sisters had become aware of the 'creature politics' of their new home, and the deal of tact which would be needed on their part to share the home of two large dogs.

Charlie Great Dane was huge. He was of the same colouring as Grey Cat's dearest Horace and Fergal, and towered way above his smaller, but much plumper, companion, Daisy Boxer. Daisy was all white in colour, with a black nose and large, dark and mischievous eyes.

The dogs lived in the farmhouse with Cara and her companion Abe, but spent a lot of their time in the yard, or in the two adjacent small fields. At those times Cara and Abe were busy with chores outside, always Charlie and Daisy would be there with them too.

The cats accepted that the dogs were primary occupants of the home which had been theirs first, and so, to avoid any offence to the dogs, or confrontations with them, they kept out of their way, and the kittens had strict instructions to do the same.

On those occasions when their paths crossed accidentally, the cats and kittens would defer to the dogs and immediately move out of their way.

Grey Cat's first encounter with Charlie had been a scary

experience for her. Aoife had just been born, when the field door of the barn opened suddenly, and in came Charlie, heading down the barn towards her.

Grey Cat was so startled at the sight of the biggest dog she had ever seen, she leapt up onto the sill of the slit window nearest to her, drawing this enormous animal's attention away from her tiny and helpless babies below.

Charlie approached her, and, to her dismay and terror, she saw he was tall enough to rest his chin on the sill beside her. She retreated further into the deep sill in the old stone wall of the barn, and he continued to regard her with one steely blue, merciless looking, eye.

She thought her end had surely come, but when he turned his head slightly, she saw that the blue eye's companion was of a soft deep brown colour and had a much kindlier expression. At that moment, a voice called out from the other end of the long barn. 'Charlie, what are you doing?'

Immediately, Charlie turned away, and trotted back down the length of the barn to join a human, whom the cats afterwards would come to know as Cara.

It was when Cara came to investigate, to see what it was that had caught Charlie's attention, that Grey Cat had first met her. Upon seeing Grey Cat, cringing on the window sill, and her helpless kittens below, Cara sent Charlie out of the barn, and, while backing away herself in order not to frighten the cat further, she told Grey Cat not to be afraid, that no-one would harm her, and she should attend to her kittens, who needed her.

To Grey Cat's immense relief, Cara had made no attempt to interfere with her kittens.

Life for the cats and kittens had since developed into a peaceful, domestic routine, and, although all the kittens did their mothers' bidding to keep out of the dogs' way, for one they still held an irresistible fascination.

With the insatiable curiosity of all young animals, Felix was fascinated by Charlie. He pursued his hobby of dog-watching so enthusiastically that, while all his senses were telling him to keep at a safe distance, invariably he found himself watching Charlie from a distinctly *unsafe* distance.

Charlie was absolutely huge, and, as he moved his great bulk around the field at the back of the barn, Felix would be watching him from one of his hiding places.

Occasionally, Charlie would look up and turn his great head in his direction, and if Felix was on Charlie's brown-eyed side, it seemed to Felix that Charlie looked friendly, but, if on the other side, the steely glare of Charlie's blue eye struck terror into the kitten's heart.

Felix spent a lot of his time trailing around after the two dogs, but, in order to technically obey his mother, taking care to remain hidden from their view.

He watched their every move and his surveillance of them kept him amused for hours on end.

One day, he was careless, and Charlie caught him watching them. 'What do you think you're doing?' said a gruff voice high above him.

Felix crouched low to the ground in terror as Charlie's huge bulk towered over him and the dog stared down at him, waiting for a reply to his question.

'N-N-Nothing, S-Sir,' said Felix.

'We saw you,' said Charlie, 'you were watching us.'

'N-Not really,' said Felix, 'I just happened to see you,' adding apologetically, in a low, guilty voice, 'and, and, I was just interested. I-I'm sorry if I've upset you.'

Charlie thought for a second. 'So, you're not spying then?'

'N-N-No, S-Sir, I should have gone away when I saw you,' adding, 'Mother has told me I must keep out of your way.'

'Mmmm,' said Charlie, 'we're not at all happy you know about you and your family moving in.' He paused, and then went on, 'They chose Daisy and me you know, but no-one invited you and your family here.'

Felix flushed hotly at Charlie's words. It was true. No-one wanted them.

'Oh dear.' said Felix, hanging his head, and gulping back his tears.

Charlie continued, 'All right then, you give me one good reason why Daisy and I should let you and your family share our home.'

Then, in his hurt and confusion, came the simple words from a humble little kitten, which touched the heart of a giant.

'B-B-Because we have nowhere else to go,' said Felix.

Charlie saw the pain he had caused, and instantly felt ashamed.

Although life had dealt him a cruel blow in his puppyhood (which afterwards had made it more difficult for him to show his true feelings), he had been blessed at birth with the same generous and sunny nature as Daisy, and now he bitterly regretted letting his jealousy get the better of his good sense and generosity.

Both he and Daisy had known what it was to be

unwanted, and he recognized how unkind he had been to the little trembling creature before him, to remind him that he and his family did not have homes of their own.

He wanted to say something kind and reassuring to him, but canine dignity would not allow him to demean himself to a cat… and a juvenile one at that!

The situation demanded some sort of response though and, while trying to look mature, responsible, and in charge of the situation, Charlie opted for a vague and thoughtful sounding remark.

'Mmmm,' said Charlie again, 'we'll have to think about that one.'

With that, he turned away abruptly to re-join Daisy, who was busy selecting play sticks from the old chewed wellie they called the DSB (Daisy's Stick Bank).

Felix ran back to the barn in a state of great agitation.

He was really worried. Suppose his foolishness had angered the dogs and they would insist upon the cats being evicted. What then? And it would be all his fault.

He knew if he told the others what had happened, they would be worried, perhaps unnecessarily, and, anyway, he hadn't the courage to face his mother and admit to what he had done.

So that the others wouldn't see there was anything wrong, he crept away into his bed, and there he waited, in an agony of suspense and anxiety, for any sign of the outcome of his foolishness. Had he known, all his fears were unfounded.

At the end of the day, before returning to the farmhouse,

Charlie and Daisy sat together in the fading sunlight, talking over the day's events.

'What do you think about this cat business?' asked Charlie.

'Oh, I don't know what to think.'

'Well,' said Charlie, 'it seems he and his family have nowhere else to go – no-one wants them.' He hesitated, not wanting to admit to his harsh words to Felix, 'and I suppose they're not really doing any harm.'

'No, I suppose not,' said Daisy, 'they pretty much keep out of our way anyway,' adding, 'but what a peculiar little thing that kitten is.'

'Yes.' said Charlie thoughtfully, 'He's very odd… but he's very polite.'

'Yes, that's true.'

'I wouldn't want to see him homeless, would you?'

'No,' laughed Daisy, 'with his looks, I think he's already got enough to contend with!'

'What do you think then, let them stay?'

'Oh, I think so,' said Daisy. 'It would be an awful nuisance anyway trying to get rid of them; you know how persistent cats can be.'

'Well, that's settled then, they can stay,' said Charlie, secretly thankful that he hadn't had to betray the sympathy he felt for Felix.

Later, as he and Daisy settled down for the night, for a while Charlie thought on the events of the day.

He flushed guiltily as he remembered the distress his harsh words had caused to that funny looking little kitten.

He thought again of how he and Daisy had both known what it was to be unwanted, and remembered his own pain at being rejected by the humans who hadn't wanted him, and who had shown it by locking him up, starving him, and hitting him.

Charlie shuddered at the bad memories which would haunt him for the rest of his life: He remembered his prison. First the cold, wet winter, and then the flies of a stifling hot summer, the thirst, the hunger, and the beatings.

Taken away from his mother and then locked away in that filthy pen, out of sight. He had thought he would die there. He could never fathom why they didn't like him, or what he had done to offend them. He had always wagged his tail and tried to make a fuss of them, to show them he was their dog – their loyal friend – but still they hated him.

Then a human he didn't know had come for him, and told him the other two were bad ones, who should never have been allowed to have him.

Bad ones, good ones, he would never understand humans. He heard Daisy's voice, sleepily saying goodnight to him.

He was content for her to remain blissfully unaware of his thoughts on the true extent of his past suffering, and that he could not forget it. He wished he could, but he knew those memories would never leave him completely.

As he did every night, he gave thanks to their Lord Provider for his deliverance from his suffering, and then pushed the thoughts of his imprisonment once more to the back of his mind.

Back in the present again, he was glad for them, and for himself, that the funny looking little kitten and his family were to be allowed to stay.

The next day, Grey Cat was surprised when Felix suddenly said to her, 'Mamma, why didn't any human choose to have us as their own cats?'

'Why do you ask?' she said.

'No reason… just something I-I… heard.'

His mother looked wistful. 'Well dear,' she said, 'there are those cats who get chosen, and then there are the others who do not.'

While she was speaking, Grey Cat was thinking to herself that from her and her sister's experience, for some it was better not to be chosen. She shuddered at the memory.

'That's not very fair,' said Felix.

'It's not a question of fairness,' replied his mother, 'it's just the way it is – and it's up to us all to make the best and the most of what we have.'

Felix went to interrupt, but his mother raised her paw and stopped him, adding, 'Don't worry yourself about it all, Felix, we are among the lucky ones. We have food and shelter here, and that's all we need.'

'Yes, but for how much longer?' thought Felix, as he reflected upon what Charlie had said to him.

Eventually, when nothing bad had happened as a result of his encounter with Charlie, Felix relaxed. He resolved though that his days of dog-watching were over – he feared that next time he might not be so lucky.

Unknown to Felix, or to the two dogs, one day fate would bring Felix and Daisy together into a very close friendship, but, in the meantime, Felix's impetuosity and sense of adventure would continue to get him into more trouble.

The Big Fir

The boy kittens spent the long Summer days of their kittenhood in boisterous rough and tumble games, all centred around the ultimate challenge of the Big Fir.

Despite the handicaps of their small size, and short, stubby legs, they had conquered most of the other trees around their home, but the Big Fir was different. They would stand at the foot of its huge trunk, and gaze upward in awe at the whorls of massive boughs above them, spiralling ever on upwards towards the sky.

In truth, the old tree was nearly 200 years old, and over 30 metres high – a majestic lone survivor of the thick pine forests which once would have grown all along that coast.

By luck – or perhaps destiny – it had survived the ravages of Man, and was unique to the extent that it was the only one of its kind for many miles around. It had become a local landmark and, for some inexplicable reason, to Felix and his boy cousins had become the focus of their frequent re-enactments of their version of 'Kitten Island' – the adventure story (set in much warmer climes) which had thrilled all boy kittens for generations.

Towards the end of the Summer which had seen Felix grow rapidly in size, to a stature half as big and heavy again as that of either of his two boy cousins, one day, once again, the boys were gazing at the Big Fir.

Felix had come out rather badly in a game of rough and tumble they had just played – Felix tripping over his own feet at the vital moment, which had then seen him sprawled on the ground at the feet of his cousins, with his cheeks flushing hotly at their giggles. He had to redeem his self respect.

After a few moments, he said casually, 'Oh that, I've already climbed it.'

Having caught the attention of the other two boys, he then went on, rashly, to lie again. 'Right to the top,' he said, and, for added effect, 'several times.'

He enjoyed the look of astonishment on his cousins' faces and began to elaborate on his imaginary exploits involving the Big Fir.

'Let's see you do it again, then,' said Maxi.

'Yes.' said Pepper, 'Go on, show us how it's done.'

Felix was shocked by the challenge, but tried to look, and sound, casual, while inwardly quaking at the thought of such a climb. He had no idea how he would even be able to reach the lowest of its boughs, which was way, way up the trunk.

Still, there was no way out of it now, and, somehow or other, he would have to do it. Playing for time to think of what to do, Felix walked around and around the base of the trunk, making exaggerated gestures, which were intended to indicate measurements, and the technicalities of his climbing stratagem, all of which had to be exacted before his climb could begin.

All the while, Felix's mind was racing.

He could pretend to faint. Certainly that would get him Mary's sympathy when she knew, but, no, it wouldn't work. He couldn't stay unconscious for ever and, when he 'recovered' his senses, Maxi and Pepper would still be there, expecting him to do the climb.

He could 'trip' over one of the exposed roots of the old tree, and 'sprain' an ankle. No, that wouldn't work either; he didn't fancy having to walk with a limp for ages, and anyway, it was tripping up which had got him into this mess in the first place.

Apart from running away, which was unthinkable because he would never live it down, he could think of nothing else.

He was on his tenth circuit of the tree trunk when his cousins began to get impatient.

'Well,' said Maxi, 'are you going to climb it, or not?'

Felix mumbled something incoherent in reply – which Pepper took to be 'Yes,' and so said to him, 'C'mon then, get started. We don't want to be waiting around here all day.'

Felix hesitated.

'Or is it that you can't do it?' teased Maxi.

Just at that moment, Felix spied Mary approaching, and, wanting to impress her with his bravery if he made the climb, coupled with the thought of losing face with his boy cousins if he didn't, he was spurred on to take one last look at the tree before making a wild leap upwards in the direction of the upper end of its lower trunk.

He landed heavily on the trunk, about 2.5 metres above the ground, finding himself spread-eagled and clinging on desperately to the thick bark.

The blow from hitting the trunk so hard had knocked the breath out of his body, and, as he hung there, gasping for breath, he heard Mary's voice.

'Oh *do* be careful, Felix,' she said, and then, 'I really don't think you should be doing this, you could really hurt yourself.'

'Yes,' thought Felix, 'and don't I know it,' but, heart thumping with the effort of hanging on, he called down to her, 'Don't worry, I'm fine.'

He knew he was anything but fine, but with Mary and the boys there watching him, he knew he had to go on.

He looked up, and saw that he was less than half way of the distance from the ground to the height of the lowest bough. If he let go now, he would not only hurt himself anyway, but also would have to bear the shame of failure, so he might just as well go on, and, if he died in the attempt, then so be it.

His breathing was short and fast, and, seeing the ground so far below, he felt dizzy and very frightened. His arms and legs were aching with the strain of supporting his weight, and he knew if he stayed in that position – hanging on desperately to the bark - he would fall.

Very carefully, he lifted one paw at a time free of the bark, and inched his way up the trunk. With his bulk, it was an enormous effort to drag himself ever on upwards and he thought his heart or lungs would burst under the strain.

He made such slow progress that, by the time he was within reach of his target, the boys below were beginning to lose interest. Mary though was still calling out anxiously to him.

'Phew,' thought Felix, as he clambered out onto the bough from the tree's trunk, 'thank goodness for that.'

He looked down, and noticed that the boys were shuffling around below in a bored fashion, so, standing up precariously on the bough, he shouted to them, to attract their attention to his feat.

He just had time to see the admiring looks on their faces, before he lost his balance, and he was then hanging beneath the bough, dangling by one paw.

He heard a shocked gasp from Mary, and the boys telling him to come down, as it was too dangerous.

'Come down,' he thought to himself, 'I wish I could. If I don't do something positive, and quickly, I'll be down with them the quick way, and they'll be scraping me off the ground.'

Under the weight of his body, the pain at the base of his claws was almost unbearable, but he *had* to hang on.

He paddled with his hind legs to try to get a grip on the trunk of the tree, but discovered he was too far away along the bough to reach it, so, the only thing for it was to stretch up as far as he could with his other front paw and try to get some sort of firmer grip on the bough.

Swinging his hind legs to and fro to gain momentum, after what seemed like a lifetime to him, his effort brought his free front paw within reach of the bough, whereupon he sank the claws of that paw firmly into the bough's bark. He then rested a minute, before he swung his hind legs up and onto the bough too.

The loud cheers and claps coming up from below from his cousins were like music to his ears.

Once he had his whole body back to the safety of the bough, he rested a minute or two, before edging carefully along it, back to where it joined the trunk, and there he sat, exhausted, with his back against the gnarled bark of the old tree, and wondering what to do next.

Below, his cousins were still clapping their hands excitedly, and temporarily Felix forgot his predicament, as they called out, 'Well done.'

It was a while before his heart had stopped thumping wildly, and he had the breath again to speak.

'*Please* come down, Felix, before you hurt yourself,' called Mary.

'Yes,' chorused the boys, 'please don't go any further,' adding apologetically, 'We're really sorry we doubted you.'

Felix knew he couldn't get down.

Clinging on coming upwards was almost impossible, and he knew it was just too far for him to be able to hold on going in the opposite direction. He would have to go down head first and his grip would not be strong enough to support his weight.

'No,' said Felix, 'I think I'll go on for a bit yet,' adding, 'It's a really great view from up here, you know.'

Feeling he had to justify his cousins' praise and faith in him, he looked around him, and saw that the next whorl of boughs was but a short, and relatively easy, climb away, so, off he went, taking care all the while to avoid the sharp points of the pine needles as he disappeared from sight into the thicker growth of the tree.

Now he was out of sight of the others, he sat down and considered his position, and, when he looked down at the trunk – almost bare of branches and footholds – he felt dizzy again.

He could continue going up, but he couldn't get down, so what was he to do?

His cousins called out to him again.

'Where are you, Felix?'

'What are you doing?'

'Are you all right?'

Felix called down to them in the most casual voice he could muster, 'I'm fine. It's great up here.'

'C'mon, then Felix,' said Pepper, 'you'd best come down before we're seen and we all get into trouble.'

'No, not yet,' said Felix, 'I want to stay here a while,' he lied. 'There's a really beautiful view here from so high up.'

Then he heard his aunt calling Mary, Maxi and Pepper.

The boys scampered off home, but Mary didn't follow until she had called to Felix and he had reassured her he was fine and that he just fancied staying a while to look at the view.

Telling him she would be back later, she too then left, and Felix was alone.

He sat for a while and admired the view, partly because it was fascinating to be able to look down on and across the harbour opposite – which looked so very beautiful with the sunlight playing on the shimmering silver blue of the surface of the water – and partly because it helped to take his mind off his predicament.

He was still musing on the beauty of the natural world – and imagining he was a look-out who could see a pirate ship sailing in – when he saw Cara appear. She was carrying a basket of wet laundry to peg out and so was heading in his direction, towards the nearby washing line.

As she came closer, he shouted for help.

At first she couldn't make out where he was, but, when she did, his heart jumped for joy to see her come close to the base of the old fir tree and look up.

In desperation, he called, 'I'm here, I'm here.'

Then, she saw him.

'Felix, what on earth are you doing up there?'

'Because I can't get down of course,' thought Felix impatiently, while continuing to plead pathetically to be rescued.

'Wait there,' said Cara.

'Where else am I likely to go?' he thought. 'Really, why do humans always state the obvious, and say such daft things?'

It was not long before he heard the clanking of metal, and there was Cara below, struggling to extend the length of a ladder to set up against the tree trunk.

With some difficulty, at last she got it to the right length, and heaved it into position against the trunk of the old tree.

Then, after making sure it would not slip under her weight, up the ladder she came, all the while coaxing him to come within her reach.

He didn't need much coaxing and, just as soon as *she* was within *his* reach, he flung himself off his perch and into her arms.

Once both were safely back down on the ground again, Felix was fussing about anxiously, willing Cara to remove the ladder – the evidence of his rescue – before any of his cousins, most particularly Mary, reappeared.

She seemed to be taking an age to shorten the ladder back down again, to be able to carry it away, and the more he tried to help, the longer it took her.

Thankfully, eventually, she left with the ladder, and so it was safe now for his cousins to return.

In the meantime, while he was waiting for them, he could amuse himself with the contents of the laundry basket Cara had hurriedly abandoned in order to rescue him!

Later in the day, when his cousins returned to the Big Fir, they were surprised to find Felix sitting in the sunshine at the foot of its huge trunk, where he was feigning sleep.

They crowded around him, demanding he tell them all the details of his epic climb. None of them was ever to know that he had to be rescued, and, although Felix had delighted in entertaining his enraptured audience with an exaggerated account of his climb, he never boasted of it again – for fear of being challenged to repeat it.

Never again; he had learned his lesson.

When Grey Cat got to know about her son's exploit, she was anything but enraptured, soundly scolding him instead for his foolishness.

Felix had been well and truly brought back down to earth.

Fox Frolics

Felix was dozing on the saddle of the sleeping red and black monster when little Mary and her brothers burst noisily into the barn.

Since the incident of trapping him in one of its rear end pouches, and battering him about, happily the monster had been well behaved.

Occasionally, it still roared into life when Abe came to wake it up and take it out to graze, but mostly it just slept quietly in its corner of the barn, and didn't object to him, or the other youngsters, perching themselves up on its saddle to rest.

It had gone out to graze once or twice a week for as long as he could remember, but, very recently, after being groomed very thoroughly by Abe, it had gone into hibernation and, although he thought Winter was a long way off yet, it didn't eat at all, spending its time instead just sleeping quietly in the corner of the barn, with its saddle very conveniently available to the young cats, whenever they wanted to use it.

Felix saw that little Mary was trembling with fright, and her teeth were chattering. Her brothers also looked very frightened, but embarrassed too.

'Come quickly, Felix,' said Maxi, 'there's a fox in the yard and he's making off with the dogs' bone.'

'Is he indeed?' said Felix angrily, leaping down from his perch. 'We'll see about that.' He ran out of the barn into the yard.

'Hey, you, what do you think you're doing?' shouted Felix.

The fox lifted his head from where he was trying to get a grip on the bone, turned around, and shouted back, 'Mind your own business, Fatty.'

Felix flushed hotly at the unkind jibe about his weight.

'L-Leave that alone, it's not yours.'

'It's as much mine as yours,' retorted the fox.

Felix thought for a moment. He could see the logic in that remark because in fact the bone belonged to the dogs.

'No, no it's not, I live here, you don't.'

'Well then,' said the fox slyly, 'perhaps I'll move in. You seem to be doing pretty well, and, by the look of you, there must be plenty of food about.'

Behind him, watching from the safety of the barn doorway, he heard Mary and her brothers gasp. The fox living *here*, they would all have to move out! Feeling confused, Felix didn't know what to say, so fell silent.

In all the excitement, until then Felix had not noticed how very skinny the fox looked, and, in truth, felt a bit sorry for him, but no, he couldn't let sentiment get in the way of his duty – he had his beloved Mary to protect – and anyway, having challenged the intruder (and in front of Mary), he would need to see it through.

'L-Let go of that bone,' said Felix.

'No,' said the fox, 'I want it and I'm going to take it.'

With that, he turned away, grabbed the bone and made

off with it up the few steps into the small field behind the barn, and was on across it, heading for the ditch on its other side, beyond which was the second field and then open countryside.

Felix ran up the steps behind him.

'Come back,' shouted Felix.

The fox stopped in his tracks, turned around, and, laughing loudly, shouted back, 'You can't chase me,' adding, 'you're a cat, and cats don't chase foxes.'

'Well, this one does,' said Felix angrily, and ran towards him.

The fox ignored him and ran on, all the while struggling to keep a grip on the large and very heavy bone he was carrying – and still with Felix in hot pursuit.

Felix was gaining on the fox.

Just short of the ditch into the second field, the fox lost his grip on the bone and dropped it, narrowly missing his own foot.

He struggled frantically to pick it up again, but it was slippery from his own saliva, and, each time he thought he had a secure hold on it, just as soon as he went to move off again, he dropped it.

Seeing Felix closing in on him, reluctantly he decided he would have to abandon the bone.

There was something very odd about this youngster, and he didn't much like the look of dogged determination on his face as he approached.

To frighten off the other youngsters had been easy enough, and who would have thought they would then fetch this... this... lunatic?

Yes, on balance, discretion looked to him to be very much the better part of valour.

Even a heavyweight youngster, like this one, was unlikely to be able to do him any harm, but he didn't fancy a confrontation nevertheless, because, at that weight, to hold him off would need a firm hand, and he would have difficulty justifying doing any damage to a juvenile of another species. Even if it were only minor collateral damage inflicted in defending himself against the youngster, he would be breaking the Code and could then well find himself in very serious trouble over it, and, by the look of this crazy youngster, who was heading straight for him at speed, there was no telling what he might do.

No, it was a shame, but he'd best abandon the bone, and make his getaway.

With that, and with one last wistful glance at the bone, he turned back towards the ditch. Then he was across it and speeding on across the second field, nimbly over the old stone boundary wall and was away into the open countryside before Felix reached the bone.

Felix was very surprised when the fox abandoned the bone and ran away, but was very relieved when he did so because, having pursued the fox on an impulse, he had had no plan of action formulated in his mind, and so had no idea what he would do when he caught up with him. Fortunately, that problem, at least, had been resolved.

He looked down at the bone.

Gosh, he hadn't realized it was so big. He was amazed that the fox had been able to lift it at all, let alone carry it all this way.

Well, no use just staring at it, somehow or other he had to return it to the yard, before the dogs noticed it was missing – and perhaps would think the cats had taken it.

On investigation, he found he couldn't open his mouth wide enough to get hold of it. A different tactic would be needed.

He walked around and around it, wondering what to do, until he found a bit of gristle on it at one end, which he discovered he could fit into his mouth and then hold it there securely with his teeth.

Next, he heaved and heaved on it until the bone began to move. He looked over his shoulder and saw it was a very long way back to the steps down into the yard, so he had best get on with it without any further delay.

By the time he had dragged the bone half of the way back, he was aching all over from the effort of pulling it along. His teeth felt as if they were about to fall out from the strain of clenching them so tightly on the piece of gristle for so long, and his back and legs ached from pulling along such a heavy weight. He had to rest.

He sat for a while, and then, getting back on to his feet, slowly and painfully, he continued dragging the bone the rest of the way.

Eventually, as he heard the bone topple from step to step down into the yard, gratefully he sank down into a heap at the top, to get his breath back, to rest his aching back and limbs, and to check that all of his teeth were still there!

It was a while before he had the strength and energy to stand up, and follow the bone down into the yard.

The yard appeared deserted, but, as he went to cross it, his cousins appeared from where they had been hiding in the safety of the barn doorway.

Although they had seen the bone roll down the steps into the yard, they had been fearful that the fox was still with it, and, supposing he to have already disposed of Felix by some awful means, they had stayed in hiding.

They crowded around Felix, all asking questions at once, and wanting to know what had happened.

Felix still felt a bit guilty about the fox, but... well he shouldn't have been so rude. Relegating his feelings of guilt to the back of his mind, Felix related a somewhat embellished account of his supposed encounter with the fox, and, in doing so, conveyed the impression to his cousins that the fox had admitted to him that he had met his match in Felix, and then had meekly surrendered the bone into his possession.

While Maxi and Pepper were busy hero-worshipping him for his bravery in the face of dire danger, it was Mary's quiet, solicitous anxiety for his well-being which made him best pleased with himself.

All in all, he was well satisfied to be the hero of the hour.

Flushed with the success of his victory over the fox, Felix strutted on across the yard ahead of his three cousins.

However, his triumph was to be very short-lived.

His cousins ran off to tell everyone what a hero Felix had been and it was not long before his mother appeared at the door of the barn.

He was still feeling rather guilty about the fox, when his mother called him over to her to speak to him.

'Felix, come here,' she said, 'I want to talk to you.'

She spoke his name so sternly, he gulped in apprehension, and ran across the yard to her. From her expression, he knew he was in trouble.

'Felix,' she said, 'I understand from your cousins that you chased away a scrawny fox this afternoon, and what I hear of your behaviour in the matter does not please me; does not please me at all.'

Felix was taken aback. 'Er, well he was very rude and he *was* stealing the dogs' bone.'

Grey Cat looked at him sternly and said, 'That does not justify your behaviour. You are well aware that, except in very exceptional circumstances, foxes are no threat to us, and I did not raise you to be a bully.'

Felix flushed hotly at her words and his heart sank. He couldn't bear to disappoint or upset his beloved mother and he had no argument – he *had* behaved badly.

'I'm told the fox looked as if he might be starving, and we countryside cat folk don't go around bullying the sick and the needy. You are fortunate, Felix, you have never known hardship or hunger – to be so hungry that it hurts to think of food.'

His mother had a far away look in her eyes now, as if no longer with him, but somewhere far away in the past, remembering deprivation.

Suddenly her train of thought was broken, and she looked intently at him. 'You have been blessed with a large, strong body, but you must remember always that you are responsible for using your strength for good, to protect the weak, and I do not expect to hear, ever again, that you have threatened any folk. Maxi, Pepper and Mary should have known better than to involve you in such silliness, but I'm answerable for your behaviour, not theirs,' adding, 'although I know my dear sister will think much the same as I do on the subject, and will have something to say to them too.'

By now, Felix was genuinely very, very sorry for forcing the fox to give up the bone and, in a quiet moment later in the day, he was to ask their Lord Provider to help the fox through his time of hardship – *and* to improve his manners!

Grey Cat continued to look sternly at Felix, as she continued, 'You realize don't you, Felix, that if the fox decides to report what has happened, you will have to appear before The Country Creatures Code of Conduct Committee to answer for your actions?'

Before he had a chance to answer, she went on to remind him that he was descended from a long, proud and honourable line, which had lived strictly by the Code at all times, and, if he had to appear before the Committee, he would be the first of her family, and the first of his father's family, to have to do so and would bring shame upon them all.

Felix's cheeks flushed hotly again under his sleek fur. He was ashamed of himself, not only for his actions towards the fox, but for incurring his beloved mother's disapproval, and perhaps bringing shame upon his whole family too.

'I-I'm s-s-sorry Mother,' he said, his stammer getting worse in his agitation.

'I know you are,' said his mother, more kindly, 'Now you go off and think quietly about what I have said to you.'

His head lowered in shame, he walked slowly back across the yard, and when he felt more composed, he went off to seek out his cousins.

Privately, Felix's mother doubted the fox would do anything about it.

They were strange and unpredictable creatures, but she had never known one to be vindictive, or hold a grudge.

From what Maxi and Pepper had told her, it sounded as if it was an older, experienced animal, deliberately teasing a younger, inexperienced one to see what he would do. She smiled to herself as she thought of how surprised the fox must have been when Felix gave chase.

Thinking on all the persecution by humans with which foxes had to contend, she doubted this one would be too worried about a young cat who could do him no harm, except possibly dent his pride a little.

She hoped not. She didn't want to see Felix publicly humiliated for a silly mistake which had been brought about by his inexperience and impulsiveness.

She felt sorry for her well-meaning impulsive son, and a bit guilty too about alarming him with talk of the Committee. However, he had to learn his place in the scheme of the country community, and it was her job to teach him.

As Felix approached, Mary, Maxi and Pepper ran towards him and crowded around him, wanting to know what it was his mother had had to say to him.

He told them what had happened, and about the

C.C.C.C.C. They were horrified. Mary said promptly, 'I will speak up for you.'

'And we will too,' chorused the boys.

His cousins' immediate, and unquestioning, loyalty to him made Felix feel better – and who on earth, he thought, could possibly resist Mary's plea of clemency for him. Nevertheless, it was many cat weeks before he stopped watching for a messenger from the Committee to arrive.

For a while after that, he thought of the fox from time to time, but he never saw him near his home, or heard of him in the local community again.

The C.C.C.C.

The Country Creatures Code of Conduct Committee met only infrequently, that is as and when it was needed to consider alleged breaches of the Country Code of Conduct.

It was presided over by Meles the Badger, Lutra the Otter, and Otus the Owl, each of whom represented an essential element of the lifestyle of any who were required to appear in front of the Committee to answer for their conduct, i.e. land, water and air. Each accused was entitled to nominate one of its own species to sit on the Committee during the hearing of its case and that co-opted committee member was matched with another of the same species who was appointed by the three presiding magistrates. Additionally, the accused was entitled to be represented in Court by an animal of its own choosing, not necessarily of its own species, and that advocate was matched against one nominated by those bringing the charges against the accused.

At the conclusion of the presentation of evidence by both advocates, the three presiding magistrates and both co-opted committee members would retire into an ante-room to decide whether the case had been proven, and the accused was guilty, or the case against the accused was insufficient, and was to be dismissed.

It was the task of all five members of the Committee to decide on appropriate punishment for the guilty.

In the case of felines, Felix's father, Horace, had been the magistrates' appointed co-opted cat, who always could be relied upon for sound advice and judgement, but, since his demise, his position had been filled, on a temporary basis, by another ageing tomcat distantly related to Horace.

Traditionally, these co-opted committee posts were handed down from father to son in the same family and, although the young Felix was unaware of the fact, he was the heir apparent to his father's position; a position which had been handed down through his father's family for generations. He was also unaware that his demeanour and behaviour had been under the scrutiny of the three presiding magistrates almost since his birth, with a group of wrens living near his home having been nominated by Otus to observe and report on his progress. To date, although now a maturing cat, and displaying the admirable qualities of compassion, kindness and fairness, his impetuosity suggested that, at present, he was still too immature in some aspects of his outlook to take up his co-opted position on the Committee.

The three magistrates continued to watch, and to wait, for the time they knew would come eventually, when Felix could be summoned to serve as a worthy successor to his father.

They hoped it would be soon, because Felix's ageing relative had a disturbing habit of falling asleep during the presentation of evidence, and sometimes during consideration of the verdict in the ante-room afterwards too, which made it very difficult for the others to present to the animals assembled a properly considered verdict when judgement was pronounced.

It had become particularly difficult during some of the more tedious and boring trivial cases which came before them, and which quickly sent their co-opted colleague to sleep, when he had to be nudged constantly to stop his loud snores dominating the Courtroom.

Just as well, thought Otus the Owl, that, as a feline, he was not co-opted to listen to the constant, and lengthy, trials of cuckoos, who were the most frequent to appear before the Court, at the insistence of those whose home nests had been commandeered to accommodate the cuckoos' offspring.

Although the cuckoos so accused always readily admitted their guilt, and were judged accordingly, their advocates also always made strong pleas of mitigation on the grounds that cuckoos could not themselves build nests, or raise young, and had been designed by the Lord Provider with the innate need to lay their eggs in other birds' nests and leave the job of raising their nestlings to those who knew how to do it.

The legitimate point was made too that if cuckoos obeyed the Court's direction to keep away from other birds' nests, it would not be long before there were no cuckoos. The magistrates usually had to quieten the aggrieved birds, and their supporters in the public gallery, at this point, because of the raucous cheers and stamps of approval at the idea of there being no more cuckoos.

Hearing cases against cuckoos had become a complete

waste of the Court's time, as it was obvious that, in the interests of perpetuating their own species, cuckoos *couldn't* obey the Court's direction.

The three magistrates were seriously considering a change in the Countryside Code in order to exempt cuckoos from the crime of violating another's home. However, they knew this move would be strongly contested by most birds and they particularly did not relish the task of convincing the meadow pipits (the birds who suffered the most from having their home nests invaded by cuckoo young to raise as their own), or the other main victims, the reed warblers and dunnocks, of the logic and wisdom of this move. The members of the C.C.C.C.C. faced other difficult problems too, which were not within their power to resolve satisfactorily.

Meles the Badger was old and very wise, and often contemplated on the one species mostly responsible for the mayhem in the countryside, Man, and that he alone was the one species they couldn't summon to appear before them to answer for his crimes against his fellow creatures.

He shuddered at the thought of the persecution of his own species at the hands of humans – and of the suffering of otters, foxes and stags.

On occasion, hounds and terriers had been summoned by the families of their victims to appear before the Committee to answer for their crimes, but, with their breeding so manipulated by Man, it was evident to all present that they had lost all sense of canine dignity and destiny. It was impossible to pass judgement on the gibbering idiots who appeared before them, prattling on about doing their masters' bidding. They didn't understand what they were doing, or why they were doing it, and were more to be pitied than punished. They were no more culpable of the crime of killing the victims, than was a bullet fired from a gun.

The hound and terrier cases were particularly hard on the magistrates' co-opted canine member, Shep, the old sheepdog. He had spent his life protecting the flocks of sheep in his care and, as he listened to the babblings of these confused members of his species, with great sadness he commented over and over again, more to himself than to anyone else, 'What have they done to us, what have they done to us?'

He kept nodding his head sadly, and the pain of what he was witnessing of his kinsmen showed in his dark eyes. He had long given up trying to talk any sense into these miscreants. They were totally unable to grasp that they were betraying their own species in the service of the dark side of Man, or that when their usefulness came to an end, Man, whom they so revered, would dispose of them too, just as dispassionately as he did of any badger, otter, fox, or stag.

No-one ever succeeded in shaking their faith in their masters, to whom, in their foolishness, they imagined they were so special.

Whenever he thought of Shep's distress over what had been done to members of his species, Lutra would ponder on the chaos Man had brought to the natural order of things.

He thought on the confusion visited upon otters by the bringing in of mink from far away across the sea.

Otters had learned to adjust to the invasion of their territory by mink, but, in doing so, all sorts of difficulties had had to be overcome, in order to accommodate the newcomers in their habitat – a habitat which, in any event, was ever shrinking in size by reason of Man's other selfish activities.

Otters regarded mink as rather odd creatures, but, although their way of speaking, with a lazy drawl, was a bit difficult to understand (and their manners left a lot to be desired), there was no real malice in them.

It was impossible not to feel sorry for them.

Through no fault of their own, they were thousands of miles from their homeland, and had no way, or hope, of ever getting back there. They were marooned for life in a foreign land, and, a lot of the time, they were homesick.

The horrifying tales they had to tell too of escaping from the hell of being shut up in small cages, and of seeing their comrades murdered so that their coats could be taken away from them, had the effect of imposing upon otters a moral obligation to help these strangers from overseas make the best of their lot in a strange land.

Not that there weren't constant arguments between the two species, but these were brought about, for the most part, by ignorance of the other's needs and traditions. With a bit of tactful diplomacy on the part of their leaders though, disputes were settled amicably, making it possible for them to co-exist, and both species shared the common anxiety of whether or not they would be able to hang on to whatever territory there was left to them in which to live and raise their families.

Lutra found it hard to believe that all these difficulties had been brought about by there actually being some exceptionally silly humans who were foolish enough to imagine that they looked better in the fur coats they had stolen than did the coats' original owners. He wondered why they didn't understand it was wrong, *and* if their Lord Provider had intended people to have fur coats, they would have been born in one of their own.

To steal them from someone else was unforgivable. He knew he would never fathom the foolishness of the human mind.

In the case of the presiding magistrates, theirs were life-time appointments. On the eventual death of an incumbent, an election was conducted whereby every member of every known population of that magistrate's species had the opportunity to vote for a successor to the post.

Most usually the selection was made from amongst their leaders, but, just occasionally, an 'unknown', with particular qualities, was put forward and elected. And so it was that the three presiding magistrates always comprised a badger, an otter and an owl. Without exception, the magistrates were exemplary in their patient understanding of the facts presented to them, and their wisdom of judgement. Except in the case of a very serious crime, usually the guilty party was required to apologize to those against whom he or she had offended, and to perform some community task for the benefit of the offended's community and of his or her own community.

Those found guilty of serious anti-social behaviour against their own, or other, species were handed over to the custodian group of their own species to be detained until they had repented of their crimes and had been satisfactorily rehabilitated. Incidents of serious crime so seldom occurred that it fell to few presiding magistrates during their term of office to impose detention.

Routinely, hounds and terriers were deemed mentally unfit to be held responsible for their crimes. They were hopeless cases and, not being able to understand that they had done anything wrong, they could not repent, or be rehabilitated. They were sent back to their masters. Thereby, the silly creatures thought themselves to be vindicated, while every other animal present knew that eventually, at the hands of those same masters in crime, they would pay the ultimate price for their witless treachery towards their fellow creatures.

One way or another, justice was served.

Past and Present

The cats noticed that from time to time, and very briefly, The Bothy looked different from the way it usually looked.

There would be cows grazing contentedly in the fields and one of two grey-haired old ladies would be going in and out of the farmhouse door, carrying buckets brimming with milk, while the other would be in and out of another door which mysteriously had materialized on the other side of the building, beside the stream.

There, in the fast flowing waters of the stream, that old lady would be washing empty buckets.

All around her, there would be groups of laughing children, sliding and slipping on the grassy banks as they tried to catch the slippery eels as they swam and wriggled their way downstream towards the sea.

What the cats didn't know of what they were witnessing was that old Nell and Nan were the last of their family to live out their lives in that farmhouse. The sisters had been born there, and continued to farm the land there until they died in the 1950s.

Even before Nell and Nan, the farmhouse had had a very long history: In the bygone days of 'old Ireland', it had been the family home of generations of their forebears, and, long before the construction in the late 19th century of the now derelict schoolhouse nearby, the large living room at the farmhouse had served as a schoolroom for the local children.

Every now and then, in a moment of time past and present colliding, the old farmhouse was brought back together with its past.

The cats saw it happen; the humans didn't.

Mary

When Mary awoke that morning, after a fitful night's sleep, she knew she had taken a turn for the worse.

She had been awake for much of the night. She just hadn't been able to settle and, keeping very quiet, so as not to wake the others, she had sneaked out of her bed several times to get herself a drink.

Now she felt really ill and was finding it very difficult to breathe.

She hadn't been well for several cat weeks, but had said nothing to her family, choosing instead to put on a brave face and appear to be her usual cheerful self. After Mori's disappearance, already her mother had enough on her mind, without worrying about her too.

Mary tried hard to suppress the loud, rasping cough, which, as she struggled to breathe, was frightening her.

She couldn't stop it, and, instantly, her mother was at her side.

'Oh Mary, my poor dear baby, what is the matter?' she asked, stroking her daughter's brow.

'I'm sorry, Mother, but I fear I'm very ill. My chest hurts and I feel dizzy.'

Inwardly, White Cat panicked at the sight of her stricken daughter, but, trying to appear outwardly calm for Mary's sake, she said to Maxi and Pepper, who also had risen from their beds and were standing nearby, 'Stay with Mary, while I fetch your aunt and cousin.'

Grey Cat was startled at the sudden appearance of her sister, as she burst in through the doorway of the barn, in great haste and in a state of great agitation.

'Oh, it's dreadful, it's dreadful,' cried White Cat to her sister, 'I think Mary is dying.'

'*What*?' shrilled Grey Cat, trying, unsuccessfully, to stay calm, 'How can this be?'

'*Please*' said White Cat, 'Come quickly.'

Grey Cat scrambled out of her bed and, in the commotion, Felix woke up and asked sleepily, 'What's going on?'

'Mary's ill,' answered his mother.

Those words were like a bolt of electricity going through Felix's body, and he left his bed in such a hurry that he tripped over his bedding and fell flat on his face on the floor.

His heart was thumping wildly as he scrambled to his feet. His beloved Mary was ill, and, judging by his aunt's and his mother's expressions, it was serious. He felt sick with anxiety.

All three cats raced out of the barn to go to the old animal house.

As Felix entered, he saw that Maxi and Pepper were sitting at their sister's bedside, one holding her paw in his, and the other gently stroking her brow.

He went forward and took Maxi's place. He took Mary's paw in his and whispered, 'Mary, I'm here with you.'

'Ah, Felix,' she whispered hoarsely, 'thank goodness, you've come.'

He smiled at her and squeezed her paw reassuringly.

Mary knew she was dying, and it was then, with Felix there at her bedside, that the urgency of the situation overcame her shyness of expressing her feelings to him.

She smiled into his eyes, and continued, 'I'm sorry, my love, I fear we don't have long left together now.'

'Oh,' said Felix, choking back his tears, 'please, please don't say that, I couldn't bear life without you.'

She sank a little deeper into her pillows and smiled again.

'Don't fret for me, Felix, in my heart I will never leave you, and, in yours, you will never leave me.'

Not trusting himself to speak, Felix nodded and continued to hold her tiny, dainty paw clasped between his two giant ones and held close to his chest.

Pepper was crying softly, and, touching Mary lightly on the other paw, he retreated across the room to where Maxi was sitting.

Grey Cat put her arms around her sister and tried to comfort her.

When Cara arrived with their breakfasts, she was surprised to find both families of cats together in the old animal house, and quickly realized there was something wrong.

By now, Mary had retreated so far into her bedding, she was all but invisible, but she responded weakly when Cara called her name.

Looking around at the others, gazing expectantly at her to do something to help, Cara told Mary she would get the cat doctor to come and make her well again, and then left the old animal house to call him.

Mary's two brothers sat in a corner of the room, staring in silent misery at their feet. They sniffed as the tears slowly rolled down their cheeks and fell with a 'plop' on to the floor.

When Cara returned, she found all the members of Mary's family crowded around her bed.

Once again, Mary responded weakly when Cara called her name.

Thinking that Mary's family could give her the comfort of her own kind that she needed now, Cara left the room, but remained nearby, pacing up and down outside, anxiously waiting for the cat doctor to arrive.

Mary's earthly life had already ended by the time the cat doctor drove into the yard.

Love Never Dies

At the very end, Mary had slipped quietly and serenely from this world to the next.

Felix was inconsolable: He wailed and wailed at the top of his voice, and sobbed uncontrollably.

He turned his distress and anger onto their Lord Provider, saying to his mother, 'H-He's mean and spiteful and h-he's taken my b-best friend away from me.'

'No, Felix,' said his mother more sternly to him than ever before, 'you must never, never say, or think such a thing again.' Before he could interrupt, she went on, 'We *all* loved Mary, and will miss her, but our Lord Provider knows what's best for us and it is our duty to have faith in him and accept his decisions without question.'

Felix went to interrupt, but his mother put up her paw to silence him, saying, more gently, 'Now, we will say no more about it. We're all very tired and upset, and need to rest.'

Felix said nothing, but, through his tears, he continued to think angrily about the being who had wronged his beloved Mary and had brought such misery to him and the rest of her family.

'I hate him,' he thought, 'and one day I will tell him so.'

His mother brushed her paw fondly once across his brow, and then left him, to go to comfort her sister.

Felix threw himself down onto his bed in despair, tears of anger and grief on his face, and, exhausted by emotion, he fell into a fitful sleep.

He slept a little at first, and then the nightmares of his first days arose from wherever they had been hiding, to come back to terrify him again.

He felt and smelt the foul breath of the night-time monster. He saw the skinny fox standing nearby, grinning malevolently at him. Then the fox turned his attention to Mary, who, with her two brothers, was standing, trembling, against the wall of the barn.

'L-Leave them alone,' shouted Felix.

'Nothing you can do about it, Fatty,' laughed the fox... 'Look behind you, if you dare.'

A loud roar deafened him. He turned and saw that the sometimes sleeping monster which ate grass had joined in.

He cried out in terror as he saw the grass eating monster trundling towards him, whirling blades at the ready.

He tried to run away, but his legs seemed to have stopped working and he fell, face down, onto the ground. He turned his head and looked up, to see not the grass eating monster, but the foul breathed one, its huge gaping mouth open and ready to envelop him. He struggled to get up, but the monster had him by the shoulders, and then he was falling, falling, backwards into that deep, terrifying black hole.

He was alone in the dark!

He shrieked in terror and heard himself screaming, 'No, no, please, someone help me,' and then... oblivion.

Then a calm fell upon him, and, when he opened his

eyes, he found he was standing on the ridge of a high hill in bright sunshine, beneath a clear blue sky.

All around him the birds were singing sweetly, the fragrance of blossom and flowers filled the air, and the cool grasses beneath his feet felt so good. 'Where am I?' thought Felix, as he looked around him at this wonderland of peace and harmony.

'Good morning Felix,' said a rabbit as it bounded across his path and away into some bushes at the side.

'How very odd,' thought Felix, 'how does he know my name?'

It was then that a shaft of intense sunlight bounced off his shoulder and continued to bounce away down the green fields he could see before him, following the course of a bubbling stream which stretched away into the distance. He followed it with his eye, and then he saw it. The most beautiful of rainbows. He ran towards it as fast as he could and it was only when he stood bathed in its kaleidoscope of colours that he noticed it was actually a staircase.

What happened next made Felix leap into the air with fright.

'So, my son, you doubt my word, do you?' boomed the great voice.

Shivering with fear, Felix answered honestly, 'Y-Y-Yes, Sir, I do.'

'Go on, my son,' said the voice, more gently.

'W-W-Well, Sir, I love Mary, and you took her from me, a-a-and that was a very unkind thing to do.'

'So, you not only doubt my word, but you think I am unkind too, do you?' said the voice.

'Y-Y-Yes, Sir, I do,' said Felix.

'Then come with me.'

Felix stood as if rooted to the spot.

'Come along, follow me,' said the voice, sternly.

'Follow who… and where?' thought Felix.

Shivering with fright again at the thought of what might befall him, he noticed that the beckoning light which had brought him to the foot of the rainbow stairs, now had begun to jump upwards, from stair to stair.

Felix had the oddest feeling and felt compelled to follow.

In confusion, and fear, behind the light he scrambled up each stair to the next – all one hundred of them – and, as he neared the top, he felt the warmth of golden sunshine on his coat.

At the top, suddenly the light disappeared, and Felix found himself alone, looking downhill, across a wonderfully green landscape, bathed in sunshine.

In the distance, he could see a group of cats, and his heart quickened as he recognized one of them to be his beloved Mary.

'M-M-Mary,' he tried to shout, but no sound came. He tried again, and this time heard his voice ring out over the wondrous land he could see beneath him.

Then, oh joy, oh joy, he saw his beloved Mary raise her head and look towards him. He thought his heart would burst with excitement, and happiness.

There she was, his darling girl, and, his impetuosity as ever conquering his fear and apprehension, he jumped from the top of the rainbow staircase and ran blindly, and at great speed, down the grassy slope beneath his feet.

He was running so fast that he was unable to stop in time and he blundered into the group of girl cats, knocking them aside like skittles.

As his Mary scrambled back to her feet, she smiled, and then laughed, saying, 'That's my Felix.'

Felix also regained his feet, and, with cheeks flushing hotly with embarrassment, as quickly as he could, he helped each of the other girls up from where he had scattered them, stammering his apologies.

Then he turned to Mary.

'M-M-M-Mary, Mary,' he said, the tears he was trying to hold back making his voice husky and incoherent, 'I've missed you so.'

Flinging his arms around her, he hugged her tightly to him.

Hardly able to breathe with being squeezed so tightly, she whispered softly into his ear, 'My darling, darling Felix, you've no idea how much I've missed you too. It's so truly wonderful to see you again.'

He was choked with tears. Gulping with emotion, and unable to speak, he held her tightly to him for what seemed like for ever, before one of her companions coughed loudly to try to get their attention, and said to Mary, 'Well, aren't you going to introduce us?'

Neither heard her.

Mary was smiling when eventually he released her.

'Dearest Felix,' she said, 'you mustn't be sad for me, I'm happier than I've been ever before.'

'See,' she said, as she did a little twirl and ran a few steps up the rainbow hill and back down again.'

She went on, 'None of you knew how bad it was

sometimes. I didn't want to worry Mother, but some nights the pain in my chest was unbearable, and I just couldn't stand it for much longer... so, our Lord Provider came to my rescue and brought me here, and, at last, I can do all the things all the other girls and boys can do, without the pain in my chest and getting out of breath.'

She smiled again, 'Please be happy for me.'

Felix regarded her solemnly. He would never have believed it possible, but Mary was more beautiful than ever.

He knew Mary was still waiting for him to say something, and, surprised at his own boldness, he said earnestly, 'I love you, Mary.'

'I know,' said Mary, 'and I love you too.'

She went on, 'It was always meant to be.'

She smiled at him, and then, gazing tenderly into his eyes, told him, 'Your place beside me here is waiting for you.' She put up a paw before he could say anything, 'Ah, but not yet,' she warned, 'you have a lot more to do yet on earth.'

He couldn't believe it. He, big, chunky, clumsy Felix loved by the sweetest, gentlest and most beautiful of all young girls. Mary had made him the happiest boy in the world. 'It's a wonderful life here,' she said, 'but I do miss Mother and the boys... and you too of course,' she said shyly.

She blushed daintily, making Felix's heart leap in his breast.

'Come along,' she said, 'Come and meet the others,' and then, taking him by the paw, she re-joined the group of pretty, giggling young girls nearby, still waiting patiently to be introduced.

'This is Felix,' Mary told them proudly, introducing her huge cousin to her new friends, and adding shyly, 'He is my fiancé and is still on earth at the present, but he has been allowed to come to see me.'

Felix hadn't been aware that they were actually engaged, but he was delighted to hear it.

The girls crowded around Felix, all asking questions at once. Did he know their families, had he seen them, and could he give them this message or that?

Felix's head was spinning with all the chatter around him and he was embarrassed by all the attention.

Mary came to his rescue.

'Now, now,' she said to the others, 'you're overwhelming him with all the questions.' The girls looked crestfallen until Mary went on, 'I'll give him a list of your names to take back with him, and, if it's possible, you can rely on him to let your families know you are well and happy. Isn't that so, Felix?' He nodded his assent.

'Oh, thank you, thank you Felix,' chorused the girls, 'you've made us so happy now.'

'Now' said Mary, 'I'll see you all later... I want Felix to myself for a while.'

The girls drifted away, and as Mary began to tell him more of her life in the place beyond the end of the rainbow, Felix realized that she had travelled through into a different dimension of time and her days there had actually begun before she had left her earthly life, and him. It was all very confusing, but all that mattered was that they were together now, and he wanted never to be parted from her again.

Efilwen

Mary began her story – and what a truly wondrous tale it was she had to tell.

She said, 'We know it as Newlife, but the younger ones here call it Efilwen.' She smiled, 'And, bless them, there is an Efilwen Kitten Club, Efilwen Puppy Club… Cub Club, Chick Club, and so on.'

Felix smiled at the thought of all those youngsters, who had had their earthly lives tragically cut short, now so very happy and enjoying themselves so very much.

'Well' said Mary, 'you can see for yourself the wonderful surroundings in which we all live.'

'Yes,' said Felix, looking around him, 'it's more beautiful even than the most beautiful of the places we have seen on earth.'

Mary smiled and said softly, 'And even better, all of us here get on so well together and so none of it is spoilt by silly arguments or being unkind to one another.'

Her train of thought went on.

'Oh, you remember the fox who came into the yard by the barn, well, I've seen him.'

Felix was alarmed. He remembered the fox's sneering threats and of how very frightened of him Mary and the boys had been at the time.

'Where is he, what did he do to you?' asked Felix anxiously.

'Nothing, nothing,' laughed Mary, 'You don't understand Felix, we're all in Newlife now, and none of us here has anything to fear from any other,' adding, 'one of my best friends here is Bob, a Doberman.'

Instantly, Felix felt jealous. Obviously, Mary had found someone else.

Seeing his crestfallen expression, and recognizing the hurt in his eyes, immediately she regretted her careless words, and hastened to reassure him.

'No, no Felix, I don't love him in the way I love you… you will always be my one true love.'

She was pleased to see his face lighten again, and added, 'I love Bob as a dear friend. He is a real gentleman, so kind and considerate, and you would be pleased to see how he is to all of us.'

Felix nodded.

Mary went on, 'His very special best friend is a Great Dane called Alfie, and they're always laughing and joking together about the time before they came to Newlife, when they hated each other, and their people had to keep them apart because of the terrible fights they had whenever they met.'

Felix found the mental picture of the clash of these two canine Titans quite alarming.

'They've told us how on one occasion Bob nearly permanently crippled Alfie with a puncture bite wound down to the bone on a front leg joint, and of another, when Alfie almost ripped off one of Bob's ears and twenty-two stitches were needed in the wounds.

Mary continued to tell Felix more about Bob and Alfie, saying, 'They can't remember now why they were so angry all the time in their earthly lives, but that anger left them immediately they arrived here.'

Mary thought for a moment and then said, 'You know, there's so much anger in the world dominated by Man. He is such an arrogant, angry creature himself, I guess he taints all around him with that arrogance and anger.'

Felix agreed.

'Anyway,' said Mary, as she went on cheerfully about the reformed Bob and Alfie, 'they dress up as clowns and 'play wrestle' now for the entertainment of the rest of us. They are *so* funny, tripping up and falling around, and have us in fits of laughter. They keep it up until they're exhausted and we're all exhausted from laughing so much.'

She giggled.

'We always know who will be winning the wrestle that day, because they take it in turns to be the winner.'

To Felix, it seemed to be a bit pointless playing a match of any kind if the winner had already been decided beforehand, but, for him, the joy on Mary's laughing face as she thought of the dogs' play wrestling, made it all worthwhile, and silently he thanked both of them for the pleasure they brought to his beloved Mary.

'Bob's mother, Jess, acts as his supporter for the bout, and Alfie has his companion Great Dane, Lily, to act for him. Both of the girls are really kind and caring, and I often have a chat with them.'

Felix still felt a little suspicious of the Doberman friend's motives, but, on the other hand, he was reassured to know that Mary had such a powerful ally to protect her from the fox, should he have a change of heart about being a Newlife member.

And what of the fox, Felix wondered, how long had he been here? He asked Mary.

'He was here before me actually, because very shortly after he saw us, he was hunted and killed by hounds – suffering a very painful end to his earthly life. I feel so sorry for him, because he's really such a jolly sort, and full of fun.'

'He didn't look very funny to me,' thought Felix, and, as if reading his thoughts, Mary said, 'He was just teasing us, Felix, and we were too young to realize it was just a game to him.'

Felix had never thought of foxes playing games, but he didn't argue.

Mary went on, 'He's really a decent sort and, when he saw me arrive, he felt very badly about his behaviour. He says that had he known I was destined for so short an earthly life, he would never have frightened me the way he did… he's always trying to make amends.'

Felix was beginning to think he had misjudged him.

'He often laughs though about the fright *you* gave *him*, and he is the only fox here who has ever been chased by a cat. Says he was so surprised at the time, he was slow off the mark and you came very close to catching him – seems you made cat/fox history with that chase!'

Felix laughed, and then his thoughts returned to the last pursuit of the fox's earthly life. 'Tell me more about him, Mary, what happened to him on that last day?' and Mary related what the fox had told her.

Tod

The fox told Mary she could call him Tod, which he explained to her was the colloquial name by which he, and his kinsmen, were known in the countryside.

Mary didn't understand.

Tod tried to explain more clearly.

'Well,' he said, 'I'm Tod,' and, pointing to a group of his fox friends standing nearby, 'and he's Tod, he's Tod… and so is he… we're all Tod.'

Mary thought how very confusing it must be for all of them to have the same name, but it didn't seem to confuse them, so she supposed that's all that really mattered.

When Tod went on to say that all foxes everywhere had the same name, she tried to picture what it would be like for her if all cats everywhere were called Mary!

She concluded that life for foxes must be very different from that for cats.

'So you see, we're all Tod.'

She nodded, and it was when she repeated, slowly, 'Tod.' and Tod and all his friends answered, 'Yes.' she decided that to have a private conversation with Tod, she would need to avoid addressing him by name.

Mary then went on to tell Felix more about her first meeting with Tod in Newlife.

Tod told her that he had spent his earthly life dodging the huntsmen and their hounds, which, in his youth, usually was not too difficult, as neither species appeared to him to be particularly bright. As he grew older though it was a different story and it became more and more difficult for him to scratch a living in the countryside while in constant danger, and under unrelenting harassment from the local Hunt.

One morning, not too long after his encounter with her and her cousins, he had been careless, and the hounds had surprised him in his bed.

Using a bit of quick thinking, he had escaped, and set off at speed, but, with so little distance between him and the hounds, from the start he had been fearful he would not be able to shake them off his trail.

He tried every manoeuvre in the Fox Manual – plus a few extra tricks of his own – but still they were hot on his heels. He was close to exhaustion when, as a last resort, he dived down into one entrance of a relative's den, which he knew to be unoccupied.

At first, he thought he had succeeded in losing them, until the huntsmen caught up with their hound servants and set others of their canine lackeys – their terriers – to flush him out of his underground refuge.

Every exit he tried was covered, and, in desperation, eventually he burst out of one, and, against all the odds, dashed on through the cordon of horses and hounds, slithered down a gulley and made it into the water of the stream at the bottom before the first hound was upon him.

To his astonishment, the hound told him it was nothing

personal, he was just doing his job, but, as the dog's razor sharp teeth sank into his flesh, he glimpsed the horses at the top of the gulley turning sad eyes away from the scene, obviously not wanting to witness the savagery taking place against one of their fellow creatures.

Then several more hounds were upon him too. He put a paw pensively to his lips, recalling that dreadful day.

'I think the dogs tried to make it as quick and painless for me as they could. They did their best, but there was an awful lot of blood, and I was so very frightened to die like that.'

He trembled at the memory, going on, 'The last thing I remember is seeing a huntsman whipping one of the dogs, who was whimpering in fright and pain. A pretty, timid little thing, who had been doing her best to keep out of it all.'

He told Mary that he didn't know it then of course, but her fate was sealed at that moment too.

'I've seen her here since. Said they took her back to kennels and she died the very same day – no good to 'em, you see, for the job they had for her.'

He put a paw to his chin as he thought about her. 'Did her a favour, mind you, as she had no lust for blood and was very unhappy there, but here in Newlife she has blossomed. She's very outgoing now, popular with everyone, and very happy.'

He went on, 'From what I understand, that's what it's all about. It's our earthly lives which earn us a place in Newlife, *but* the bad ones go to a dark, secret place instead. Few of *them* ever get to leave *there*…' The fox smiled, and went on, 'so, while the victims of their cruelty and greed are here, in the sunshine, relaxing with friends and kin, they stay in that awful place. Justice at last!'

Mary's heart went out to Tod, and to the brave little hound who had defied her human masters, and then had paid with her life for it.

Tod said, 'You must meet her. She's a caring little thing and so quite unsuited to the job for which she had been bred by... by... those *monsters*.'

He trembled with emotion as he thought of them.

He took a moment to compose himself, and then apologized to Mary, saying he was still having difficulty in controlling his anger against huntsmen. They had been responsible for the deaths of most members of his family, and his abiding memory of them in the last moments of his own earthly life was of them pointing at him, and grinning.

He said to Mary, 'Can you imagine it, *grinning* to see me in that state – terrified and facing a horrible death – what sort of creatures do that?'

He was getting angry again, 'I hate 'em, I hate all of 'em,' he said, going on, 'They really are nasty bits of work. Never could understand our Lord Provider allowing them into our world. They spoil everything they touch. They're nothing but trouble.'

Mary could understand his anger, and thought how dreadful it must have been for him and for his family, imagining herself in his place, and of losing her own beloved family to such savagery.

'Not all humans are huntsmen though, you know,' she said quietly.

'Can't trust any of them, believe you me.'

Mary had known only two humans and they were nothing like the shocking ones Tod was describing.

'I wish you could have known our Cara and Abe – they would never have hurt any animal.' Tod was puzzled by this confusing description of a species he had mistrusted and hated all of his life.

'Really, Tod, if they had been around at the time, they would have tried to rescue you from the hounds.'

He didn't really believe it, but he made allowances for the naivety of such a young, inexperienced little cat.

'Well, have it your own way, but all I know is that I never want to be around another human, ever again.'

Mary had known he was unconvinced by her arguments, immediately making a mental note to talk to him again whenever, and wherever, she could, to try to convince him that it was unjust to condemn all humans for the actions of a minority of them – a minority whom she thought must lead very unfulfilled lives if their idea of fun was torturing and killing their fellow creatures.

It was later on, Mary told Felix, that she was to meet the little hound bitch who was killed because she wouldn't attack Tod, and Tod was right, she was a sweet and gentle soul, who, after her unhappy earthly life, and untimely death, so very richly deserved the happiness she had found since in Newlife.

Eternity

By the end of the story of Tod's last day on earth, Felix's eyes were glistening with tears for him, and for the little hound bitch.

When Felix thought of what the fox had suffered at the end of his earthly life, instantly he felt sympathy for him and wished he could apologize for having chased him. Mary said though that Felix had been accorded an exceptional privilege in being allowed a visit into Newlife before his time, and therefore his visit would be all too brief as it was, without sacrificing any of their time together to seek out the fox. She would relay Felix's apologies to him, which she knew would delight him and his fox friends.

Felix felt relieved to have made amends, albeit by proxy, until such time as he would be able to tell the fox personally of his remorse.

Still thinking on the fox, Mary said wistfully, 'I've still not been able to convince Tod that there are good humans too,' adding, 'Strange really, because we only get to see the good ones here.'

Felix looked puzzled.

'Oh, I see you don't understand,' said Mary, 'Well you see it's only the good ones that get to see us.'

Felix still looked puzzled, and Mary smiled, 'Well, to

come here, they have to be sponsored by at least one of us.'

'Oh I see,' said Felix, 'so those who have been neglectful of or cruel to their fellow creatures on earth don't get sponsored.'

'Yes, that's right,' said Mary. 'Oh I do wish you could see though how wonderful it is to see animals here reunited with their people,' she laughed, 'and sometimes it's quite a crowd, I can tell you, because some humans get sponsored by lots of the animals here – all those they have known in their earthly lives.'

Felix smiled.

'It can get to be quite a party,' said Mary happily.

'No-one is ever sad or lonely here, Felix,' said Mary more seriously, 'and already I've been given lots of new friends.'

She smiled, 'It was Lily who introduced me to Puffin, Ben and Bess.'

'Who are they?' thought Felix. He asked Mary.

'Oh, like Lily and Alfie, they're old friends of Cara too,' explained Mary. 'Puffin is a pony and has been here for absolutely ages, and he spends a lot of his time with Ben and Bess.'

Before he could ask if they were ponies too, Mary went on, 'They're Great Danes, and they look *so* like Alfie and Lily, sometimes it's hard to tell them apart, and between the two boys, it's really just their difference in size.'

She turned to Felix, eyes open wide, 'Alfie you see is big, but Ben is enormous and, can you believe it, at one time, he was less than one centimetre shorter than the tallest dog in the whole world!'

Felix was impressed.

Mary thought for a minute, 'Come to think of it, that must have been a good while ago now, because he and Bess have been here for a long time too.'

She smiled as she thought of them all, before going on, 'Together, Puffin, Ben and Bess know just about everyone, and they've been so kind and helpful to me in getting to know who's who here – *and* the stories *they* can tell!'

She smiled again.

All the while, Felix had been watching her, the love of his life, the expression on her face telling him clearly how very happy she was in this world, a world so very far apart from his own. While he regretted he had not been sharing this wonderful world of happiness with her, he was grateful to their Lord Provider for granting her the company of so many good, kind friends, who cared about her and made her so happy.

He was content. She was happy, so he was happy.

Mary continued her description of life in Newlife:

'Then, every Sunday, The Battery Hen Choir sings for us in concert.'

Felix was incredulous.

'*Hens – singing*?' he asked.

'Oh yes,' said Mary. 'They've had such sad and miserable earthly lives, poor dears, shut away from the sunshine and the sweetness of fresh air, that when they come here, they want to sing for joy, but, being chickens, they don't know how.'

Mary laughed at Felix's obvious astonishment at the idea of singing hens.

'Oh I know it's hard to believe, but everything here really is very different from the way things are on earth,' she smiled again, 'and it's all so much better, for everyone.'

Felix was confused. He had heard how horrible life was for those hens that humans kept caged up in sheds, in the dark, and he was sad and angry for their suffering, but how did they get to sing in Newlife?

'Ah,' said Mary, 'I can see you're wondering how they get to be able to sing.'

Felix nodded.

'Well,' said Mary, 'that's where the songbirds come in.'

Felix still looked puzzled.

Mary continued, 'The songbirds have known the freedom of the countryside, when song was an intrinsic, very important part of their earthly lives. They feel so sorry that the battery hens who arrive here have never known their families, or the sheer joy of living which they themselves had enjoyed on earth, they give them singing lessons – and now some of the hens have the sweetest of singing voices imaginable and they have their own choir.'

Felix was astonished, and then, thinking on it, he was delighted to discover that the meek actually inherited something superior to the earth.

Mary went on to describe the particular hens she knew personally, and of how the Choir's concerts always ended with everyone's favourite hymn – 'All Things Bright and Beautiful, All Creatures Great and Small'. She said, 'We all love the words, particularly the bit about The Giver of Life having made us all, and not just humans, as so many of *them* choose to believe.'

She smiled happily, 'And we all cheer, stamp our feet, and join in for the chorus.'

'I wish you could hear the Choir,' said Mary wistfully, 'but they perform only on Sundays, so it won't be possible for you to go to one of their concerts until you are sent here to be with me for ever.'

'Why can't I stay here with you now?' asked Felix.

'Oh, no, no Felix, my love, you have to wait your appointed time to be summoned, and that won't be for a long while yet for you...' adding miserably, 'much as I so want you to stay.'

'So, there's no way I can stay now?'

'No...' and, seeing his crestfallen expression, Mary added, 'I'm so, so sorry, but that's the way it is, and has to be.' She paused, 'But I will be waiting for you, remember that.'

How could he forget it, he thought, it was now the most important, and most wonderful thing in his life.

Seeing the hint of sadness still lingering in his eyes, Mary said with as much cheerfulness in her voice as she could muster, 'Anyway, let's not think about that today. Let's make the most of enjoying the time we have together now.'

Felix smiled. 'Yes, you're right, let's make the most of now.'

For a while, they sat silently side by side, holding paws.

Felix looked at Mary's dainty paw clasped in his, remembering the last time he had held it so, and of how she had then slipped away from him. Now he wanted never to let go of her paw again.

Mary looked into his eyes and smiled as he squeezed her paw. She knew what it was he was thinking, and said softly, 'Trust me, Felix, one day there will be no more partings, and we *will* be together… until the end of time. You'll see.'

Felix tried to smile back, but, inside, he was aching at the thought of having to say goodbye to her again.

He couldn't trust himself to speak, so opted for squeezing her paw again. Mary was content; she knew he understood.

In truth, she dreaded their parting again too, and, in an effort to reassure him she was happy in Newlife, she broke their silence with, 'So you see, Felix, there is no anger, fear, greed or cruelty here, just trust, friendship, and eternal happiness for us all.'

Felix nodded.

'It was your love for me, and mine for you, which brought you here. It was so sad for both of us that I was called away too quickly to have the time for proper goodbyes to be said, and you needed to see me, Felix, to content your mind that I am well and happy…' she smiled, 'which I am, and now you can live out the remainder of your earthly life free of the pain of grief for me,' and then added, shyly, 'And I needed to see you too Felix, so, very, very much.'

Before he could say anything, she went on, 'I thought my heart would break when I was taken from you.'

Felix's heart leapt with joy at her words – to know for sure that he indeed meant so much to Mary. It was beyond his wildest dreams and made him the happiest cat in his, or her, world.

'Now we have had this brief… wonderful… time together,' said Mary, 'each of us can continue again, but in contentment of our state, knowing all is well with the other, until the joyous time for us arrives, when we will be together again, for ever, in this wondrous place.'

It was then that Felix was startled by the loud clanging of a bell from somewhere nearby.

'What's that?' he asked.

'Oh my love, my love,' said Mary, 'you have to go now, that's the Dream Visitors' Bell,' and, taking him by the paw, said, 'Quickly, I will take you back to the rainbow.'

Felix thought for a moment. '*Dream* visitors – do you mean to say that this is all just a wonderful dream?' he asked miserably.

'No, no, not at all,' and, to convince him, 'It's true my love for you, and your love for me brought you here to me. You're really here. You're real... and so am I... see,' she said, squeezing his paw affectionately, 'I'm just as real as you are.'

Felix's eyes glistened with tears at the thought of leaving her and, seeing his distress, she squeezed his paw again and said softly, 'Now, we *have* to go.'

At the top of the rainbow hill, Mary smiled at him, and kissed him goodbye. 'Think of me,' she said, 'I will be waiting,' and, knowing how forgetful he could be, added, 'And don't forget to give my love to Mother and the boys.'

Then she was gone, and he was alone at the top of the rainbow hill.

He was looking around him, when he heard the booming voice there again with him. 'Now,' asked the voice, 'would you wish Mary back with you, in pain and distress, merely so you could have her there with you?'

Felix answered, 'N-No, of course not... and I-I'm sorry

I doubted your word and thought you unkind,' adding, with grave sincerity, 'I see now, you do know best, and it is not for any of us to question your decisions.'

The voice didn't answer immediately.

'I-I-I'm really sorry, Sir,' said Felix, 'for doubting you.'

The booming voice was softened, and chuckled, 'You are forgiven, my son. You are young and have a lot to learn.'

'T-Thank you, Sir,' said Felix humbly.

The voice went on, 'My son, you will live a very long and happy earthly life, but you have a place here when your time there is done.'

Then the voice was gone too, and Felix knew it was time for him to go, and he set off back down the rainbow staircase, to return into his earthly life.

Resolutions

When Felix woke, he felt good. He knew Mary was happy and so he must be happy too.

One paw was still tightly clenched around the scrap of paper Mary had pressed into it as she left him. He opened his fist, and, to his astonishment, the paper, with the names of Mary's new friends on it, no longer existed. The imprint of where it had been was still there, but, in its place, was a glistening pinch of what some would know as 'fairy dust'.

He felt badly that he would not now be able to tell the girls' families that they were well and happy, but he was content too to know that he had brought happiness to the girls in their thinking he would be able to do so, and, as he now knew, one day they would be able to tell their folk themselves.

It was his Mary who had handed him the paper, and so he would now treasure the 'fairy dust' which had taken its place. He wrapped it carefully in a small piece of tissue paper and placed it under his pillow – where it would remain for the rest of his life.

Felix's mother was astonished at the change in her son, and Mary's mother and brothers were even more astonished when he told them, 'Mary is more beautiful than ever and is very happy. She asked me to give you her love.'

Nature's Colours – Pink for a Girl

Immediately after Mary died, Cara had gently wrapped her tiny still form into one of her bed blankets, and then she and Abe had laid her to rest in the soft earth beneath a hydrangea bush, which every year bloomed in profusion with pink flowers, and stood in a sunny corner beside the old animal house in which Mary had made her home.

They were unaware that her entire family was watching from secret hiding places nearby, with tears slowly rolling down their cheeks.

It was to puzzle Cara thereafter, in the days, weeks, months, and years which followed, to see Felix so often just quietly sitting close to that hydrangea bush, with a solemn, far-away look in his eyes.

Rejection and Redemption

As soon as the kittens had been old enough to understand, they had understood from their mothers, and had accepted, that one day they would leave, to start a new life in a new home.

That day for Maxi and Pepper came at the end of the Summer, not too long after Felix's epic climb.

Felix had hoped that he and his boy cousins would set out on that exciting new adventure together, but it was not to be.

Unfortunately for Felix, Maxi and Pepper's new people couldn't accommodate a third, and so, as his two cousins left to go to their new home in Killarney, Felix stood in the yard, waving goodbye to the pals of his kittenhood, until they were out of sight.

Then, he was on his own again, and anxiously awaiting the day when 'his' new people would come and take him off to his new life too.

He spent a lot of time imagining what they would be like.

Several people came to see him, but, despite his best efforts to look appealing (opting for an exaggerated grin and unfortunately producing the reverse effect), invariably his looks let him down and always they left without him.

He was still growing fast and had yet to blossom into the exceptionally fine and handsome cat he was to become, and so, at the time he was waiting for his new home to materialize, he was chubby, still looked rather shapeless, and had odd looking eyes, one of which appeared to be more intent upon regarding his nose than following the direction of gaze of its partner.

Very much he was an ugly duckling in waiting for transformation into a beautiful swan – a fact which, unfortunately for him, was consistently overlooked by all those who came to see him.

They were quite startled by his weird facial expressions and all, without exception, then decided he was 'not quite' what they wanted.

It was their loss that they didn't recognize in him the most affectionate of natures and the kindest of hearts.

He was mindful that Maxi and Pepper were adopted by the first people who saw them and he was hurt and humiliated at being rejected so many times.

Once again, Grey Cat's heart ached for her only son.

Each time his hopes of a new home were dashed, she felt his pain and disappointment.

She tried to comfort him.

She told him of how he had to remember that humans were unpredictable, capricious creatures, and who knew what went on in their silly heads? Most of what they did made no sense at all to any of their fellow creatures, and the extent of their actual intelligence could be measured by the extent to which they busied themselves destroying their own habitat – the habitat on which they depended for their own survival! They were alone in the world in that foolishness of purpose.

Grey Cat tried to reassure him that his time would come, but, in her heart, as he did in his, she knew that there was not going to be anyone to offer him the chance to prove himself.

She felt anger at those who had rejected him – anger which, in part, was brought about by her own lingering feelings of guilt and shame.

She knew it was the second time he was being overlooked, solely because of his looks.

The people who now had rejected him had been unable to recognize his true worth – in precisely the same way as she had failed him when he was born.

She thought with shame on how, at his expense, she had chosen to preoccupy herself instead with her other handsome son and two pretty daughters. It was unfair then, and it was unfair now.

Remembering that she had been taught a hard lesson for her unjustness, she hoped that those now who had hurt and humiliated poor, kind-hearted Felix, also would come to regret it.

For his part, Felix was utterly demoralised at his lack of success in securing a new life for himself, but stoically faced the truth – no-one wanted him!

It was to be a time of great uncertainty for him, in not knowing what the future held for him, but he contented himself with the life he knew, in the home he knew and loved.

It was not to be too long before his fortitude in the face of adversity was to be rewarded and their Lord Provider sent him two new companions.

Another View Too Far

It was in the time between the departure of Maxi and Pepper and the arrival of his two new companions, that the fiasco of the farmhouse roof occurred.

Certainly there was no way he would make another attempt on the Big Fir, but the farmhouse roof looked to him to be a much easier climb and he reckoned that the view across the harbour from there would be much the same as from the Big Fir – and so it was he began to plan his next climbing exploit.

The old farmhouse across the yard from his home in the barn was a long, low building, with small windows set in one metre thick stone walls, and immediately above them were the eaves of a steep pitched roof of thatch.

Ever since the episode with the mysterious man in the bobble hat, the roof had aroused Felix's curiosity.

He had spent long hours, watching intently as the bobble-hat man worked, first stripping the old thatch down to the original scraws draped over the roof rafters. The scraws were then left where they had been placed two and a half centuries before, but the old thatch was carted off into one of the fields and piled up into the most enormous heap Felix had ever seen.

That was fun too, and he took some time out every day

178

from his vigil of watching the new roof taking shape, to explore the delights the old thatch had to offer.

As he burrowed into it, to his young nostrils the smells were wonderful. A whiff of bird here, a whiff of rat there, and, everywhere, the lingering sweet smell of turf smoke, mingled with a tantalizing mix of reminders of long forgotten meals.

He spent many happy hours exploring the delights of 'The Heap'.

He did notice though that the old thatch made him itch – and it was when his mother discovered he was alive with fleas, that she forbade him to go near the heap again.

Its attractions were such that Felix was tempted to disobey her, and so it was fortunate for him that not long afterwards it was turned into an enormous bonfire and reduced to a pile of harmless ashes.

Then he was in trouble with his mother for leaving blackened paw prints all over the barn floor, and his bedding.

The thatcher was a young man, small in stature, usually with a cheery smile showing below the technicolour woollen hat he kept pulled down low on to his brow as he worked. Felix watched, mesmerised, as the loosely attached bobble on the hat danced and twisted in the breeze which blew along the ridge of the roof.

The bobble-hat man spent seven cat months living at the farmhouse while he replaced its roof with new reed.

During the whole of this time, Felix had watched from daybreak to dusk, fascinated to see the bundles of reed being handed up to the thatcher on his precarious perch on the naked roof. Felix saw that he kept his supply of scallops in a welly-boot quiver, and he waited patiently each time to hear the knock-knocking of the wooden mallet, as the thatcher carefully hammered home each bundle of reed into position and then secured it there with his scallops.

One morning, there was a bit of added excitement.

Felix noticed that Abe, who was assisting the bobble-hat man, was limping badly on one leg, and appeared to be in pain. He heard him complaining to the man in the bobble hat about having something called lumbago. Felix had no idea what lumbago might be, but, if it hurt and made you limp, then certainly he didn't want it!

He watched Abe struggling to collect the bundles of reed from the store, and then carry them, two at a time, up the ladder and on to the scaffolding from which the man in the bobble hat was working at the time.

As ever, Felix remained fascinated to see the way in which the bobble-hat man carefully placed each bundle into its allotted place, and then expertly hammered it home with the wooden mallet.

Every now and then, the bobble-hat man would shout, 'Scallops,' and then it would be a bundle of scallops carried up to him instead, and the bobble-hat man would continue to hammer in each one of them – just like giant hairpins – over the bundles of reed to hold them securely in place.

It was when Felix was about to leave his observation post, and go in to have his lunch, that it happened.

As Abe went to step up on to the scaffolding from the ladder, suddenly he gave a sharp cry of pain and then lost his balance.

Felix's eyes widened in horror, as he saw him tumble

back down to the ground again, still clutching the bundle of scallops, and then lie there, motionless, for several minutes.

'My goodness,' thought Felix, 'he's killed himself.'

He continued to watch anxiously, to see what would happen next.

The bobble-hat man didn't notice at first, but then looked down, and, after shouting, 'Are ye all right?' several times, he turned away from the roof and was about to come down from the scaffolding to investigate, when Abe stirred. He stood up slowly, and shakily told the bobble-hat man that he was okay.

The bobble-hat man didn't answer. Instead, turning back to his work, he shouted, 'Scallops,' and his now very badly limping assistant scrambled awkwardly on to the ladder to deliver them.

Felix decided to forego his lunch. He didn't want to miss any further drama which might develop, but although, with his tummy rumbling with hunger, he watched for the rest of the day, nothing further untoward happened.

The day Felix chose for climbing on to the new roof of the farmhouse was the day Abe had left early in the morning, to visit family in England, and would be away from home for several days.

During the morning, Felix had watched Cara busying herself with chores about the yard, and he had tried to help with the watering of the boxes of geraniums which adorned the sills of the windows of the farmhouse facing the yard.

By the time all were watered, Felix had droplets of water all over his coat, and Cara's feet and ankles were wet from Felix accidentally knocking over the watering can and spilling its contents.

When Cara left to go indoors to change into dry socks and sandals, Felix waited, but quickly became bored with waiting for her to return.

He was looking around for something else to do to amuse himself, when he noticed a small piece of thatching reed break free from the farmhouse roof and then float on the breeze, to land on the opposite side of the yard. There, the breeze whirled it around and around.

He gave chase, and spent a few frantic minutes chasing in circles, trying to tap the reed with his paw. When it consistently evaded him, he became bored again – that is until he thought of from where the reed had come.

He decided on the spot that it *must* be a sign. The roof was beckoning to him to explore!

After looking over his shoulder to make sure Cara was still indoors, he trotted briskly back across the yard and then on under the gate to the foot of the short wall which supported one side of the corrugated iron roof of what once had been an animal house attached to that end of the farmhouse.

Rising up from the lower level of the yard, there was a sloping grassy bank up to the foot of the wall and so, to gain access to the roof of the old animal house at this point was but a leap of no more than a metre or so from the top of the grassy bank and over the top of the clumps of montbretia growing against the wall.

He landed on the corrugated iron with a loud bang, which rang out across the yard.

He waited, expecting Cara to appear to tell him to come down off the roof, but, no, there was no sign of her, so she couldn't have heard the sound of his landing.

Okay then, he was still unobserved, so it was onwards and upwards!

He had planned to clamber up from the sloping roof of the old animal house on to the thatch above the eaves of the farmhouse, but, when he tried this manoeuvre, he found it was impossible to get a grip on the smooth, slippery surfaces of the reeds.

He dropped back down on to the corrugated iron. This would need a different tactic. He stood back and studied the problem. If the reed was unclimbable, then he would have to tackle the chimney stack instead. This rose up through the corrugated iron roof on which he was standing, all the way up that end gable of the building until it stood about half a metre above the ridge of the roof, and was topped by one chimney pot.

He moved forward and touched the surface of the chimney stack.

Ah ha, it was covered in rough plaster – now *that* would make for a much easier climb. Something to grip. He looked up and saw that it was not too difficult a climb, but it was quite a distance up the chimney stack to the top.

Well, he'd best get started then, before Cara appeared and made him come down. From a standstill, he leapt upwards and landed with the claws of all four paws firmly gripping the plaster. He inched his way upwards, for what seemed like a lifetime to him, until, breathless and tired, he was holding on to the pot at the top of the chimney stack.

As he had supposed from below, from his perch he could step down on to the ridge of the roof. To his surprise, he discovered that the ridge wasn't reed, but was flax – and he was to find its tough, wiry stems to be a firmer and easier surface on which to walk.

He stepped down lightly on to the ridge and set out along its length towards the seaward end of the building.

He felt quite pleased with himself, but, as he advanced, he soon discovered there was one element of the enterprise for which he had not bargained. While it was just a very light breeze dancing around the yard below, up here the wind was very much stronger, and, the closer he came to the seaward end of the roof, the stronger it became.

Midway along, there was an obstacle. Another chimney stack, topped by twin pots. He found he could not climb around this squat stack, because, to do so, would mean slithering along the reed thatching at the height where it met the flax ridging. The roof was very steep and he knew the reed to be too slippery for him to risk venturing down on to it.

He looked again at the stack and the chimney pots. The pots were close together, but he thought that if he breathed in, he would be able to squeeze his body through the gap between them.

Next, he was up on the top of the stack, and trying to squeeze through the narrow gap between the pots. There was one panicky moment, when he thought he was stuck, and, as he paddled wildly with his feet to free himself, he had horrible visions of being trapped there, like the filling in a sandwich!

Once he was through though, it was on along the roof ridge, and it was as he neared the seaward end, that two things took his breath away:

Wow, what a view! Just as spectacular as that from the Big Fir, but without swaying branches and foliage obscuring any part of it.

He clung there to the ridge of the roof, gazing in awe of the panorama before him. A breathtakingly beautiful scene of the harbour, which at low tide, as it was at the time, was fringed with a dazzling expanse of golden sand, meeting the shimmering silver blue of the sea.

It was then he began to realize fully just how strong was the wind coming off the sea. He could scarcely breathe, and it was all he could do to resist the strength of the wind which was vigorously ruffling his coat and buffeting his body, as it gusted around him on his precarious perch.

Reluctantly, he decided he had best not stay any longer, for fear a sudden gust dislodged him and sent him rolling down the roof on to the yard below.

Taking one long last look at the harbour, and committing every detail of it to memory, very carefully, lifting only one paw at a time, he turned around, until he was facing back along the ridge.

With his eyes firmly fixed on the opposite end of the roof ridge, he set off.

He had not gone far before he heard Cara calling his name. He looked down, and saw her looking around the yard for him.

Just at the moment he precariously leaned over sideways, to peer down, he slipped and nearly lost his footing.

Margaret Rice

His scrabbling feet dislodged a piece of flax, which then drifted away from the roof. The wind had caught it and, after spinning it around and around, then dropped it down on to the yard at the feet of Cara.

She picked it up and, puzzled by its sudden appearance, she looked up at the roof. Then she saw him.

'Felix,' he heard her shout, 'I don't believe it; not again. What on earth are you doing up there?'

He had no answer, so opted instead for an appealing, timid expression, to get her sympathy, so that she wouldn't be cross with him.

Creeping slowly, with his body pressed down close to the flax, he continued along the ridge, and, still in some trepidation, he arrived at the chimney stack with the twin pots.

As he climbed up on to the stack, and began to squeeze himself between the pots, he heard Cara shout again.

'Felix, don't you *dare* get stuck.'

'Of course I'm not going to get stuck. I'm not stupid,' he thought irritably, but to keep Cara on his side, he flashed her an exaggerated smile, which she then mistook for fear, and, from then on, was really worried he would panic and fall.

Undaunted, it was then on through the pots, and on along the ridge, until he was back at the big chimney stack.

It was at this point he realized there was another major snag to this expedition also for which he had not bargained.

While scaling the chimney stack to get up on to the roof had not been a particularly difficult climb, going back down it again was an entirely different enterprise. Holding on to the chimney pot beside him, he stood on the top of the stack, and looked down. It was a sheer drop, which he

knew would be impossible to negotiate head first. The only other option, of jumping down, was far too risky and dangerous – it was way too high and he knew if he tried to jump down on to the corrugated iron roof, most certainly he would injure himself, perhaps seriously. He would have to be rescued. Then, the most dreadful thought struck him. Although Cara was aware of his predicament, this time she wouldn't be able to hoist a ladder to rescue him. The sloping roof of the old animal house couldn't support a ladder, and he knew, from watching the man with the bobble hat, that the roof thatch was too fragile and unstable to take the weight of a ladder.

He began to panic. He couldn't get down – and no-one could get up to rescue him! Oh why, oh why, didn't he learn the lesson of the Big Fir?

He heard Cara shout again.

'Stay there, Felix, don't move.'

By now, he was just about frozen with fear anyway, so he meekly did as he was told, and clung desperately to the pot at the top of the chimney stack, while with eyes tightly closed, he prayed for divine intervention to save him.

Then, he heard a noise, and, opening his eyes again, he looked down, to where Cara was scrambling up on to the old animal house roof, slipping and sliding on its slope, trying to get a grip.

Eventually, there she was, at the bottom of the stack. Not exactly the miracle for which he had been praying, he thought, but it would do.

She called up to him.

'Now, Felix, start to climb down.'

He shook his head.

'Don't be a silly boy,' she said, adding, with a lot more confidence than she felt, 'and don't worry, I'm here to catch you if you fall.'

He was too scared to move.

She tried again, and, finally accepting he had no other option, he succumbed to her reassurances and coaxing, and, in trepidation, began his descent.

Almost immediately, he started to lose his grip, and was flailing about wildly with his feet, to try to slow his descent as he began to slither down the chimney stack, out of control.

He knew his only hope was Cara, who was there below him, with arms outstretched to break his fall.

As he lost his grip completely, and was dropping down through the air, shrieking loudly in terror, she positioned herself to catch him, but the force of his fall as he landed in her arms, knocked Cara backwards and, clasped together, they then rolled over and over down the roof, before bouncing over the montbretia and falling on to the grassy bank.

There, Cara lay winded, but, shielded in her arms until they had hit the bank, Felix had fared better.

He jumped up, and stood over her, watching her anxiously for signs of life.

At last, he heard the sharp intake of air, as Cara began to get back her breath.

Felix breathed a deep sigh of relief. He knew he would never have had the courage to admit to his mother that he had killed Cara!

Slowly Cara rose to her feet, shaken and dizzy, but unhurt.

Felix fussed around her legs, doing his best to apologize, and then sat meekly at her feet as she scolded him soundly for his foolishness, and told him, in no uncertain terms, that he was *never* to go near the farmhouse roof again.

He adopted a suitably chastened expression, but his mind was elsewhere, thinking all the while that although the farmhouse roof now, unquestionably, was out of bounds to him, nothing had been said about the roofs of any of the other buildings!

The Prodigal Daughter

The alarming experience of the first time he had explored beyond the immediate confines of his home, when he was a small kitten, did not dampen Felix's curiosity, or his enthusiasm for exploring, both of which were to remain with him well into adolescence and beyond.

Early on in his excursions, he had met a pretty silver tabby girl cat, who told him she was his cousin and that her name was Mori, and, because his sense of direction still left a lot to be desired, she had given him detailed directions on how to find his way back home.

He continued to run into Mori from time to time, and, on those occasions when he didn't chance upon her, always it took him much longer to get home!

He had told his family of his occasional meetings with his cousin and, while it was an enormous relief from anxiety for White Cat to know for sure that no harm had come to her missing daughter – and much as she longed to see her again for herself – she knew it had to be Mori's own decision to come home to her mother, and not for White Cat to go and seek her out.

Felix understood why this was so, but always made sure he relayed to his Auntie White Cat every detail, however trivial, of his meetings with Mori, and it was in that way - with the services of a very willing go-between – that White Cat was kept in touch with her daughter and could be content to feel she remained a part of her life.

Whenever Felix saw Mori, on parting from her, he would say, 'Well, you know where we are if you ever need us,' and he continued to hope that Mori would return home.

On the last occasion she and Felix had met, Mori had stood and watched her cousin hurrying off on his way home, staring after him until he disappeared out of sight over the brow of the hill.

Then she sat down and thought about what Felix had kept telling her of what life was like for him and the rest of his and her family. How they had shelter, with warm, comfortable beds, and good nutritious food provided for them each day, while they still had their freedom to roam in the countryside as and when they wanted to do so. On wet days they could stay indoors, in warmth and comfort, with plenty to eat.

She considered her own position.

Much of the time she was cold, wet and hungry, as food and shelter became more and more difficult to find, and she knew that, before too long, she would have a family of her own to feed too.

She still had her strong instinctive fear of humans, but Felix had assured her that their carer was kind and considerate, and she had come to know him well enough to know he would not lie to her.

She asked herself, did she have the right to inflict her own life of hardship and deprivation upon her kittens too?

She knew now the difficulties her own mother had faced,

and flushed at the thought of the harshness and unjustness of what she had said to her the night before she had run away.

She sat and thought about it for a long time, before deciding that she would put her dilemma 'on the long finger' and wait for her kittens to be born, when she would then reconsider the situation.

And so it was that the arrival of her two kittens – Mori Junior and Arti – changed her life for ever.

It was raining heavily the day Mori returned home.

Since the departure of Maxi and Pepper, Felix and his mother had been spending more of their time around at his aunt's cosy home, knowing she was lonely without her two boys, and was missing them.

As the weather would be keeping all of them indoors that day, they had planned to spend the whole day together.

Felix sat quietly, listening to the rain beating down on the roof of the old animal house, while his mother and aunt chatted together. He was bored, but he knew his aunt needed their company, and so he was content to be there. They were family, they had close ties to one another, and it was right that they should be there for each other when they were needed.

Suddenly, something caught his aunt's attention and she hurried across the room, to look out of the door.

'I don't believe it,' she murmured to herself, her eyes wide with surprise.

'What is it?' enquired Grey Cat.

White Cat didn't answer, but repeated, slowly, 'I don't

believe it,' and continued to stare from the doorway, her gaze firmly fixed on something outside.

Her daughter was standing there, bedraggled, with two tiny kittens tumbling around her feet, both oblivious to the soaking rain.

'Hello, Mother,' she said, and White Cat, struggling with the conflicting emotions of wanting to hug her daughter and of wanting to slap her, being unable to decide between the two, settled on the middle route of aloofness.

'You had better bring your little ones inside out of the rain, before they catch cold,' she said.

Then she stood back and watched her errant daughter meekly bow her head, as she brought the two enchanting tiny grankittens across the yard and into the doorway of the old animal house to meet their grandmother.

'This is Mori Junior,' said Mori, indicating the pretty silver tabby girl kitten standing shyly at her side, 'and that is Arti,' pointing to the dark-coated tabby boy kitten happily skipping towards his grandmother.

Young Mori overcame her shyness and joined her brother, and, as they ran up to her, looking up with eyes bright and shining with excitement, White Cat brushed their cheeks gently with her paw and said, 'Welcome, dears,' and then, relenting a little towards her daughter, said to her, 'It's good to see you back,' adding, 'Felix and his mother are here. Come in and meet your aunt.'

'Uncle' Felix

Felix adored his tiny, playful second-cousins, and they adored him.

In their company, he was back into kittenhood again, as he took them around his home, showing them where, and how, he had played there when he was a kitten.

He was their hero and they watched him with shining, adoring eyes as he related all the, somewhat exaggerated, adventures of his own kittenhood.

The family had welcomed the two tiny strangers into their home, and the babies' mother looked on contentedly at their happiness, but with a wistfulness about her too, which made Felix feel sorry for his cousin.

What had passed between his aunt and his cousin since her return home, he didn't know, but he saw that his aunt had warmed towards her daughter gradually, although it appeared there would remain a degree of awkwardness between them, that neither could entirely overcome.

Felix liked everyone to be good friends and, in his ever kind and helpful way, he went out of his way to be friendly towards his cousin at every opportunity, and continually to 'sing her praises' to his aunt.

In that fashion, life settled back into routine.

Mori

Mori was missing!

Immediately, Felix felt a sense of dread.

Had she been unhappy after all with them and had run off again? If she had not, where was she, what had happened to her?

As the news of Mori's disappearance spread, neighbours began arriving at The Bothy to offer to help look for her and, as the old animal house became more and more crowded, pandemonium broke out with everyone milling about and everyone talking at once.

White Cat stood back from the others and blamed herself bitterly for her daughter's disappearance, wringing her paws together in her anxiety. In her desperation, she even allowed herself to think on what she knew the others would be thinking... but, no, Mori would never desert Mori Junior and Arti; no daughter of hers would leave her kittens.

Everyone was preoccupied with his or her own reaction to the crisis, until it was Felix who noticed that his cousin's two small kittens were in a corner, clinging to one another, and weeping softly.

'Stop, everyone,' shouted Felix above the din, 'Calm down, and think of the little ones.'

A silence fell immediately, and the two babies ran across

to Felix, who put his arms around them, immediately comforting them and reassuring them all would be well, and their mother would be found.

Neighbours White Face, Blackie, and Prancer volunteered the information that each of them had glimpsed Mori briefly on the evening she had disappeared, but it was at a distance, and they couldn't say to where she was heading. They hadn't seen her since. Patrick and Cassidy, and their partners (both named Tortie) said they had seen Mori the day before that, but they too had not seen her since.

None of the other neighbours had seen her recently and so none could throw any light at all on her disappearance.

Over the next three cat weeks, the family and the neighbours split up into search parties to scour the countryside to find Mori, but always leaving one family member at home to babysit the kittens, both to comfort them and to prevent them from going off in search of their mother, as they wanted to do.

Three cat weeks had now passed, and still there was no sign of Mori. It didn't look good.

Mori saw the speeding car just too late.

On a balmy Summer's evening, she was strolling, to take in the sweet perfume of the hedgerow flowers and to enjoy the peace and tranquillity of the countryside.

After all the trauma of her life on her own, she felt good. She was back with her family, and her two little ones, Mori Junior and Arti, were safe and happy, surrounded by members of their own family to watch over them. She felt good, indeed very good.

She wandered along, letting her thoughts dwell on how fortunate she had been.

First she thought on her precious little ones, with whom she had been blessed, and then on her dear mother, who, in spite of everything which had passed between them in the past, had welcomed her back into the bosom of their family. She was indeed a lucky cat, to have come through those dark days of separation into the light which was guiding her to a bright future.

Her train of thought was broken abruptly by the loud roar of a racing engine.

She turned, and saw the vehicle she had heard and that it was about to hit her. She flung herself to one side, towards the ditch, but felt a searing pain in her left hip.

She had not quite made it to safety, and had been struck. As she comprehended that fact, her body was bowled over by the force of the blow. The momentum of her rolling body caused her to hit her head, hard, on the edge of the road, and then everything went black.

When Mori awoke, it was to the gloom of the dead of night. Her head ached badly, she couldn't see properly, and her leg was hot and throbbing. She tried to stand, but fell back, agonised by a burning pain in her left hip.

Then she was very frightened. She was alone in the night, unable to stand, or walk, and very vulnerable to danger.

She lay there for a while, considering her predicament. She had to find shelter, so somehow she *had* to move herself away from the exposed position in which she was lying.

She peered into the gloom and looked around her. Across the road from her, she could just make out the outline of an old stone wall, with large trees overhanging it from its other side. To the right of the wall was a gap, through which she could crawl to shelter, *if* she could make it that far.

She cried out with the pain of her hip as she struggled to position herself to face the wall opposite.

She panted from the effort, but, after satisfying herself that she was facing in the right direction, she rested a while.

Before setting out, she double-checked her position, to make sure she had not confused the direction, and then heaved herself forward using her forelegs, with the injured hind leg trailing along behind, and its companion scrabbling helplessly beside it.

The pain was unbearable, but she knew she had to keep going, to get across the road as quickly as possible, before another vehicle came by.

After what seemed to be a lifetime of pain, she had made it to the opposite grass verge. There she relaxed her front legs and sank down to rest, before having to make the final painful effort to get through the gap, to the other side of the wall, and the safety of the trees.

When she felt ready, once again she heaved herself along, and on through the gap in the wall to the shelter of the brushwood beneath the trees against the wall.

Exhausted, and in very considerable pain, she sank down, and then came blessed oblivion as she once more lapsed into unconsciousness.

She didn't know how long she lay there, drifting in and out of consciousness, but, at times, she thought she heard her mother calling to her. She whispered, 'Mamma', and imagined she was back at her mother's breast, with her mother murmuring softly to her, while keeping her warm and safe.

Once, when she fancied she heard her mother's voice, she tried to shout, 'Mamma, I'm here.' but her mouth and throat were dry and the cry which came out was but a hoarse whisper, which no-one could hear, but herself.

Time went on, and she felt herself beginning to drift away from her earthly life. Tears rolled down her face. What a way for it all to end. Neither her two precious darlings, nor her dear mother, or any of the rest of her family, would ever know what became of her, and, even worse, maybe they would think she had run away again, and abandoned them.

She sobbed in despair. She couldn't move; she could do nothing to help herself, and all there was left to her now was to await her fate.

She drifted into sleep.

She awoke some time later and again began to think of her family, whom she would never see again. Suddenly, the voice of Cara, calling her name, penetrated her dismal thoughts. She heard the voice getting closer to her, and tried to cry out. Again, the sound which came was very faint, but then she heard the voice ask, 'Mori, is that you?'

'Yes, yes,' she wanted to shout, but no sound came.

'Please, please, don't give up and go away,' thought Mori, and, just then, the brushwood around her rustled and parted, and, joy oh joy, there was Cara come for her.

'Oh, Mori, my poor, poor baby, whatever has happened to you?'

Mori trembled and whimpered as she was then gently lifted from her hiding place, and carried back to the safety of the farmhouse on the homestead where she and her family lived.

She was saved!

Mori's family and neighbours had searched for her and called until they were exhausted and they had heard Cara calling Mori's name as she searched the entire area for her too.

As darkness was beginning to fall on the fourth cat week, and the family had returned home from another fruitless search, suddenly they heard Cara's voice in the yard outside. They looked out and, praise be to their Lord Provider, Cara had found Mori and was carrying her gently towards the farmhouse.

Felix took the initiative and crossed the yard, to look in through one of the windows, and there he saw his cousin lying in a makeshift bed, being fed with liquid from a long bottle thing with a plunger on the end.

His cousin tried to stand, but fell back on to the bed, crying in pain.

One of her hindlegs looked very odd indeed. It was hanging limply from her hip. Felix re-joined the others, who were waiting anxiously in the barn for news. 'Well, she's alive,' he said, 'and Cara is treating her.'

'What's wrong, what's wrong?' they chorused.

'Well, I think she has an injured leg. She can't stand on it and she's in pain.'

At that, White Cat was wringing her paws in anxiety again, and Felix said to her, 'Try not to worry, I'm sure she's getting very good care,' and then to the others, 'All we can do now is sit and wait for news.'

Shortly afterwards, there was the sound of a car in the yard. They all ran to the windows to look out.

Yes, it was the cat doctor arriving. They recognized him from the time he had been called to treat them when they had had influenza. His clothes had smelt funny, but he had been kind and gentle with them and had made them well again in no time at all.

During the period of Mori's recuperation from her accident, Cara saw to it that she had at her disposal a cosy covered bed in the porch of the farmhouse. There, Mori was able to relax, and take full advantage of her hospital accommodation to get well.

Mori's only worry was for her little ones, but each day either Felix, or their grandmother, took young Mori and Arti to visit their mother, and so she was content, knowing that they were happy and were being well cared for. She shuddered when she thought of what would have become of them, and herself, had Providence not intervened and she had been persuaded to return home before her accident.

Once Mori was beginning to be able to use her injured leg again without pain, on sunny days she could be seen sitting on the window sill of the porch in the sunshine, but it was not until she was pronounced to be fully fit again that she re-joined her family in their home across the yard.

Happily, other than limping slightly on her injured leg, she was left with no other ill-effects from an accident which had brought her so very close to a premature death.

Mori Junior and Arti

The day Mori Junior and Arti left home, and he had to say goodbye to them, Felix would remember as being one of the worst days of his life.

In truth, it was breaking his heart to see them go, but, for their sakes, he put on a brave face, smiling and joking with them about all the adventures they would have, before hugging both of them close to him, so that they couldn't see the tears in his eyes, as he said goodbye to his dearest little friends.

Felix hugged both his little second cousins again before they left for their new home, waving goodbye to them then until the car carrying them away was out of sight.

So kind and soft-hearted, there was a lump in his throat as he returned to the barn to join the others. It all seemed so lonely and quiet without the two boisterous youngsters around.

In the way of mothers since the world began, Mori was sad, but resigned to having to let her babies go.

Over the cat weeks which followed, Felix missed them dreadfully, but, trying not to show just how much he missed them, he cheered and comforted himself with happy thoughts of all the wonderful adventures they would be having in their new surroundings.

He had never left home, and so always he had imagined how very exciting it would be to do so.

It was fortunate for big, kind hearted Felix that he was never to know during his earthly life what actually befell his two tiny companions who meant so much to him, for it would have distressed him deeply.

Very shortly after arriving at his new home, Arti was allowed outside, in unfamiliar surroundings and without supervision, and not knowing that the garden gate led on to a road, being naturally curious to see what lay beyond the gate, innocently he ventured out.

He was struck by a passing car, which did not stop.

It all happened too quickly even for him to see what was about to hit him and so, fortunately, he knew no fear or pain at the moment his short earthly life came to an end so abruptly.

Mori Junior spent some time trying to locate her brother, and was lonely and fearful in their new home without him.

One day, not too long afterwards, and as her mother had done before her, she disappeared, and was never heard of again.

Felix remained in blissful ignorance of their fate, but Cara was very distressed to learn what had happened, and blamed herself bitterly for what had proved to be a bad choice of home for the two youngsters. She prayed that wherever Mori Junior was now, she was safe and happy.

Had the cats been aware of Arti's death, they would have known that he was safe and happy in their Lord Provider's care, beyond the end of the rainbow.

Friendships Forged

One sunny day in early Autumn, Felix came across Daisy Boxer, lying with her head on her front paws.

This was not unusual, but he could see that her face was crumpled, and was wet with tears, and quite obviously she was very distressed.

'Er,' said Felix nervously, 'whatever is the matter... er... Daisy?'

Never before had Felix addressed Daisy by name.

He, and his family, always had regarded Charlie and Daisy as the A.I.C. (animals in charge), normally waiting to be spoken to first, and Felix followed his responses always with a respectful 'Sir' or 'Ma'am'. However, he knew instinctively that, on this occasion, it was not deference, but friendship and kindness which were called for, and, in the circumstances, 'Ma'am' was far too impersonal.

Daisy looked up and blinked at him through her tears. 'It's Charlie,' she said, 'he's gone.'

'Gone, gone where?' thought Felix. 'Er... I saw him only this morning,' he said, 'sitting in the yard in the sunshine. He can't have gone far and, if you will let me, I will help you look for him.'

Despite her distress, Daisy smiled indulgently at him through her tears.

'What a funny little creature he is,' she thought, 'always so keen to be kind and helpful.' 'No, you don't understand,' she said, 'he's gone for ever; he died at lunchtime today.'

Her eyes were glistening with tears for him.

'Oh, no,' thought Felix, 'this is truly dreadful.' He knew how much Charlie and Daisy meant to one another.

Remembering the unbearable pain when his own beloved Mary had died, he said, softly, 'I am so very, very sorry.'

Daisy nodded and went on, 'It all happened so quickly. During the morning he told me that he felt a bit odd, but I expect you know how much he loved his food, and I thought it would be indigestion from gobbling it down too fast.'

The tears began to roll down her face again. 'He rested the rest of the morning, and then he said he had a fierce pain in his chest... oh, it was so awful, then, then, he looked towards me, tried to speak again, and then collapsed... and, and' she choked back her tears, 'he was gone.'

She had difficulty going on. 'After all those years together,' she said tearfully, 'we didn't even get to say goodbye. It's so unfair...'

'Yes,' said Felix, 'I thought that way once... but I was wrong.' He went on, 'We have to remember that our Lord Provider, The Giver of Life, knows what's best for us and I *promise* you that Charlie is still with you.'

He continued before she could interrupt, 'You love him, the way I love Mary and one day your love will bring you together again in another place, for you to see for yourself that he is well and happy.'

Daisy hadn't a clue what this odd little creature was on about, but he was *so* sure.

Maybe there was something after all in the rumours of his being a bit of a mystic, and she felt strangely comforted.

Felix sat down quietly beside her. He knew how she felt. He had thought he would die too when his Mary was taken from him – and now it was the same for poor Daisy.

Daisy was sobbing, and he said nothing for a long time, until her sobs began to subside, then he said, softly, 'You *will* see him again, you know.'

Daisy turned her tear-stained face to him, and asked, 'What did you say?' He repeated it.

'But *how* do you know?' she asked miserably.

'Well,' he said, 'listen to this.'

Then, slowly and carefully, he told her all about the rainbow staircase, of seeing Mary, and of how she was waiting for him.

'So you see,' he said, 'Charlie will be there, waiting for you.'

Daisy sat there, wide-eyed, taking it all in, and, when he had finished his story, she said, 'Thank you, Felix, from the bottom of my heart.' She paused and then went on, 'It's strange it should be you helping me through this, because I was not always thinking kindly of you, and, at first, I resented you for being here.'

'You needn't have been jealous of us cats, you know,' said Felix, 'because always Cara has loved each of us for who we are – you for being you, me for being me, and so on.'

Daisy nodded.

'And, as you will never be me, and I will never be you, we're not competing against one another, and so there's never been any need to worry.'

'Thank you, Felix, you're a good sort, and you've made me feel a lot better,' said Daisy, more cheerfully.

Daisy had been very surprised to find this odd little creature's chatter so very reassuring, but he truly *cared* and that in itself was comforting.

In a rush of gratitude for the solace he had brought to her, she blurted out suddenly, 'Will you be my friend now I am alone?' and Felix answered simply, 'I've always been your friend.'

They sat side by side in silence until the last of the sun's rays had sunk below the horizon.

Each felt truly at ease in the other's company.

When Daisy rose eventually, to go indoors, she turned to Felix and, regarding him solemnly with her large dark eyes, she said simply, 'Thank you.'

Felix nodded.

In the days that followed, although Daisy missed Charlie dreadfully, she had accepted what Felix had told her, and knew her own destiny had yet to be fulfilled, and then she and Charlie could be reunited, to be together for ever.

As a large, powerful dog, she had never considered a friendship with a cat, and, quite honestly, felt a little embarrassed about how much she enjoyed Felix's company. They had long chats together about anything and everything, and she was surprised to discover that cats were not the cold, unfeeling, calculating creatures she had been led to believe, but were caring, wise and knowledgeable.

He, in turn, knew she wouldn't want other large dogs to know of their friendship, and so they had an unspoken pact that, if the occasion demanded, they would sham a dog and cat chase, with a lot of show barking, but all the while making sure she never caught up with him!

One day, Daisy sought out Felix. 'Seems they're getting me another companion,' she said.

Felix's heart sank. Did this mean the end of his and Daisy's friendship?

As if reading his thoughts, she went on, 'Don't worry, that will not change anything, and we will still be good friends.'

Felix sighed with relief, feeling as if a great weight had been lifted. His friendship with Daisy meant a lot to him.

The appointed day arrived for the new dog to make his debut.

Daisy was waiting anxiously in the yard, not knowing what to expect. Suppose she didn't like him, or he didn't like her, what then?

She need not have worried. Just at that moment Abe's car came into the yard. The door of the car opened, and, to Daisy's astonishment and delight, out tumbled one of dear Charlie's kin – a tiny Great Dane puppy.

Daisy ran forward to help him to his feet.

'Sorry,' he said, 'I didn't realize my legs were too short to reach the ground, and I lost my balance.'

'Sorry!' thought Daisy, 'Why was this baby apologizing? He was gorgeous. A little steely grey coloured barrel on short legs, with the most heavenly cornflower blue eyes,' and she knew he was all hers to look after. At last, a baby for her to mother. She just wanted to hug him and kiss him, right there on the spot, and she couldn't wait to get started on his upbringing.

From his vantage point, just out of sight in a corner of the yard, Felix felt a twinge of jealousy as he saw Daisy greeting the newcomer so enthusiastically. Then he reprimanded himself for his selfishness. He knew that, in the way there was cat chat, specific to cats, so too there was dog talk, and he was pleased to see his friend Daisy so happy again in the company of one of her own kind.

Daisy looked down at the puppy sitting at her feet, gazing up at her with those amazing blue eyes, waiting to be told what to do. She smiled at him, and he wagged his little tail vigorously with delight. She liked him, she liked him!

Then Daisy looked across the yard, to where Felix was watching, and smiled at him too. In his hiding place, Felix was pleased his friend had remembered he was there.

Daisy looked down again at the puppy, still waiting for orders, and said to him, 'Come along with me.'

Meekly and obediently he rose to his feet, and allowed himself to be ushered into the warmth of the farmhouse.

Daisy was anxious to get him indoors. The weather was cold and damp, and babies so easily became chilled. She was responsible for his welfare now, and she would make sure no ill or harm came to him.

In his hiding place, Felix began to feel the chill of the fading day too and, having seen for himself that his friendship with Daisy was safe, he made his way back to the barn, to the warmth of his own family home.

As Daisy had assured him, Felix had had no need to worry about their friendship, and, at the first opportunity, she introduced the new puppy to Felix.

She announced with pride to Fionn, 'This is my good friend, Felix.'

Felix's face flushed red under his coat. He felt proud at Daisy's words, but embarrassed by the attention.

'Now,' said Daisy, 'there's something you have to understand, Fionn. Whatever you might hear from other dogs later on, although Felix is a cat, he and his family are special, and, on no account, are they to be harassed.'

Fionn nodded, and she went on, 'From time to time, you might see me chasing Felix, but this is for reasons you won't understand, and is nothing for you to worry about, but, under no circumstances whatsoever are you *ever* to tell any other dogs we have cat friends. Do you understand?'

'Yes,' said Fionn, wondering what all the fuss and secrecy was about.

Being too young to have learned the prejudices of species, and races, Fionn was only too happy to be friends with everyone, and was blissfully unaware that there was a tradition of cats and dogs being on opposing sides. He was missing the company of his mother and his seven sisters, and just wanted to be liked and accepted in his new home.

He felt he was expected to say something, so he came forward and said to Felix, 'I hope you will want to be friends with me too,' and Felix said simply, 'I'm sure we will be great friends.'

And so it was that an unlikely trio of friends was born, and long, long after dear Daisy had left her earthly life to join her beloved Charlie, Fionn remained a true and loyal friend to Felix and his family, and they to him.

Justice

Over time, Grey Cat had become increasingly worried about the unwanted attentions of a tomcat, who had tried to accost her whenever she left the safety of her home, forcing her to take every precaution to ensure she stayed well away from him.

He was an ageing, uncouth and vulgar lout, who leered at her, and every other female, at every opportunity. He took no pride or interest in his appearance, and, as a consequence, always his coat was ragged and dirty, and, when he grimaced with what he appeared to imagine to be an alluring smile, two rows of blackened stumps of teeth were exposed. The thought of having him anywhere near her made Grey Cat shudder.

After her darling, gentlemanly and handsome Horace, why that horrible dirty lout would think she would have any interest in him was a complete mystery to her, but, from his veiled threats, she knew he was a danger to her and to all the family living at her home.

One morning, she was in the yard when, to her horror, the tomcat squeezed under the old iron double gates which led out into the lane, and ran across to her. Before she could do anything, he had her by the arm, and was dragging her towards the gates.

She screamed, and, pressing his face close to hers, he told her to 'Shut up.' His breath was foul.

She knew that smell! This was the one who had taken away her babies and done away with them.

At the time they were abducted, she had vowed that however big and dangerous their killer might be, if ever she had the chance to do so, she would tear that creature limb from limb, or die in the attempt.

She rounded on him, spitting, biting and clawing, but, he was bigger and heavier than Grey Cat, and all the while he held her away from him, he was laughing and jeering at her attempts to harm him.

She needed help.

She screamed at the top of her voice for Felix.

Still the tomcat laughed. 'Like mother, like babes,' he jeered, 'and a fat lot of good it did any of *them,*' he said, 'and I doubt that the fat one you have left will do much better.'

He grasped her even more tightly, saying, 'Now then, Mrs High & Mighty Grey Cat, it's no use struggling; put on as many airs and graces as you like, but I'm as good as you and you're coming home with me, whether you like it or not,' adding, in a frighteningly menacing tone, 'I want kittens, and you're going to have them for me.'

The thought of that dreadful brutal creature warping the minds of innocent little kittens into his evil ways filled her with horror. No, she would never let that happen. She would kill herself first.

She renewed her screams for help – and then help was on its way.

'Help, help,' heard Felix, and, running out into the yard, he saw his mother struggling in the grasp of a scruffy tomcat, who had her firmly held by one arm, and was dragging her across the yard towards the gates.

Grey Cat was very frightened, and, in desperation, shrieked again for Felix – and then there he was, her big brave boy running across the yard towards them.

'L-L-Leave my mother alone,' shouted Felix.

'Clear off, Fatty,' the tomcat shouted back, 'and mind your own business. This is between your mother and me and if you know what's good for you, you will keep your distance.'

As Felix moved closer, he caught a whiff of that foul smell, and despite his anxiety for his mother, a chuckle of disbelief bubbled up from nowhere. *So,* the monster which had terrorised him in his first days, and had haunted his dreams ever since, was actually no more than this scruffy looking tomcat who was scowling at him across the yard.

'L-L-Let my mother go, y-y-you murderer,' shouted Felix, 'or, or it will be the worse for you.'

'Clear off,' the tomcat shouted back, 'or you will see just what I can do to irritating little fatties like you.'

'Be careful, Felix,' cried Grey Cat, 'he's a really nasty piece of work.'

Felix narrowed his eyes at the tomcat, and advanced.

'I'm not scared of the likes of you,' he said, 'I'm not little and helpless any more, like I was when you took away my poor little brother and sisters.'

With that, Felix caught the tomcat by one shoulder, and spun him around with such force that the tomcat lost his grip on Grey Cat, and, as much to his own surprise as that of the tomcat, he punched the lout squarely on the nose.

The tomcat heard Felix shout, 'Take that,' just before the blow from Felix's right fist landed so hard on its target, it knocked him to the ground.

Felix was very surprised to see him go down because, never having hit anyone before, he had had no idea of his own strength, and so didn't know he could deliver such a powerful blow.

He was astounded when the weight of the punch knocked the tomcat clean off his feet. 'Now,' said Felix, standing over the by now whimpering tomcat, 'you leave my family alone; you've done enough harm already.'

Felix expected, and was prepared for him to retaliate, but, in the way of bullies since the world began, this one too was a coward. He lay where he had fallen, whimpering and dabbing his bleeding nose.

'Do you understand what I'm saying to you?' said Felix.

'Yes, yes,' whimpered the tomcat, 'I never meant your mother any harm.'

Felix stared at him. 'Go on,' he said.

The tomcat went on, 'I knew your father before he met your mother and I was jealous when I saw them so happy together. It wasn't fair she loved an old cat like him, and I had no-one to love me.'

Tears of self pity began to roll down his face, 'When he died, I thought that was my chance to get her to want me, so I followed her here but then she was busy with you lot and kept avoiding me...' he paused, 'and then, and then, well you know what happened, it all got out of hand.'

Despite the terror and tragedy the tomcat had brought to Felix's family, momentarily Felix felt a pang of pity for him. It was almost unbelievable that this scruffy, smelly wretch had been foolish enough to entertain the ridiculous notion that he could get Felix's elegant, beautiful mother interested in him, and Felix began to see that, in a way, the tomcat was a victim too – of his own twisted craving for affection, which eventually had driven him to kill innocent kittens.

Felix couldn't help but feel sorry for him if he had never had anyone to love him, but, nevertheless, he needed to make sure that he never troubled his mother ever again, and so, without any hint of pity in his voice, he leaned down to whisper menacingly into the tomcat's ear, 'If you *ever* set foot in this yard again, you can be sure you will not leave it again in one piece. Do you understand?'

'Yes, yes,' said the tomcat, 'and I'm sorry, I'm sorry, I'm really sorry for what I've done.'

'Now go,' said Felix, 'before I change my mind.'

The tomcat scrambled to his feet and, without a backward glance, hurriedly made off under the gates and ran away out of sight.

Felix turned to his mother, who had slumped down on to the yard. He could see she was crying for his brother and his sisters.

He ran to her, to comfort her.

'That, that awful creature killed them,' she sobbed.

'Yes, I know, I know,' said Felix quietly. He put his arm around her shoulders which were shaking with her sobbing, 'but nothing we can do now can bring them back to us...'

'But I failed them,' cried his mother, 'I wasn't strong enough to make him pay for what he did to them.'

'No, you didn't fail them,' said Felix. 'You know violence isn't the answer, you've told me that often enough.' He went on, 'I had to hit him, to make him let you go, and I could have gone on to do him some real harm for what he did to Fergal, Aine and Aoife, but you know well enough that you wouldn't have wanted me to do that, and bring myself down to his level.' He paused, 'Now isn't that true?'

She nodded.

'And if you had done the job yourself, would you have wanted his blood on your hands?' He answered his own question, 'No, of course not.'

His mother looked up at him, 'Now,' said Felix, 'come, dry your tears and come in and rest for a while to get over your ordeal.'

'Yes,' said Grey Cat quietly, 'of course you are right.'

With Felix at her side, Grey Cat started off slowly across the yard, and then she stopped. She thought for a minute and then said, '*But* you know there *is* one thing we can do, and that's to report him to the C.C.C.C.C.' She paused, 'That's at least a small bit of justice at last for my poor babies. Their killer is now known, so his crime against them can be recorded, and, as a 'Wanted' cat, he will know no rest anywhere from now on.'

'Yes,' agreed Felix, 'that's what we should do,' He smiled at her, 'and it's the right way to do things.'

He smiled again, 'And from what you have told me of Father, I think he would have been proud of you today.'

Grey Cat smiled to herself, thinking it was not she who

had earned Horace's approval today, but his fine son, who had rescued her, and had routed a murdering bully, while exercising restraint, and respecting the Country Creatures Code of Conduct… and all in the course of just a few minutes!

The next day, Grey Cat contacted the C.C.C.C.C. and reported the tomcat's attempted abduction of her, and her certainty now that it was he who had abducted and harmed her three kittens.

His description was circulated, but, despite some initial reports of sightings, the tomcat couldn't be found – and was never seen, or heard of, again.

Bachelor Life

As time went on and he became an adult, with his fine physique and sunny personality, Felix became the most eligible bachelor in the neighbourhood.

Grey Cat went out of her way to make sure her son noticed the qualities of any young girl cats whom she considered could make him a good, loyal partner, but, as the years wore on, she knew he was never to take a partner and know the joys of parenthood.

She knew where his heart lay, and one of his strongest qualities, like that of his dear father, was loyalty, and so she knew she had to accept he would remain loyal to the love of his life, always, to the exclusion of all others who might have made him happy. Nevertheless, it grieved her to see him remain alone.

For his part, over the years Felix saw cats come and go in the neighbourhood, and some were pretty girl cats, among whom there were those who went out of their way to show him they found him attractive.

When they eventually succeeded in catching his attention, he was polite and friendly, but his interest in them never went beyond a casual friendship.

His mother continued to worry about him being alone. She wanted him to know the comfort and companionship of partnership, and, with his kind, playful and loving nature, he should have a family of his own to raise.

Often she thought, wistfully, that had Mary lived on, what a handsome couple that sweet, gentle creature and Felix would have made, and what truly beautiful grankittens she would then have had around her, to fuss over.

She would sigh, knowing it was never to be now, and it was not for any of them to question their lot in life. It seemed such a waste though. She knew Felix would make a wonderful father, and, with his kind and generous nature, no kitten could ask for better.

She continued to urge him to take a partner, and continued to worry about him being alone, but, in her heart, she knew she had to accept the situation, and be proud to have such a fine son, of such strong character.

Often as she looked at Felix, she would think that, although he was clad in a sleek black coat with bold white markings, and Horace's had been white figured with black, how very like his dear father Felix was in character and bearing. She just knew Horace was as proud of him as she was herself.

She considered herself to be so very lucky to have been blessed with such a fine partner, and equally fine son.

Felix remained resolute. He would remain single. He belonged to Mary, and she to him. However pretty and charming others might be, none could ever replace her in his affections. He knew Mary was waiting for him, and he would never let her down.

And so it was that the handsome bachelor remained a bachelor throughout the whole of his earthly life.

Time To Say Goodbye

Felix was worried. His mother wasn't well.

The rigours of her early life had left her with a chest condition which troubled her every Winter, but this time her bronchitis had persisted into Spring. She looked very pale and tired. She had no appetite and just picked at her food.

Cara had taken her to the cat doctor and she had been taking the medication he had prescribed for her. Nothing seemed to help though and Grey Cat had felt herself getting weaker and weaker.

This was the day she knew it was her time, and, when she looked at her son, his anxious face watching her, and willing her to get well, a tear slid down her cheek at the thought of leaving him.

'Felix,' she said at last, 'you must be brave. I will always be with you dear wherever you are.'

She smiled at her fine son, brushed her paw lovingly across the top of his head, and then closed her eyes for what was soon to be the last time.

She looked so small and helpless as she lay there on her bed. Felix was so upset to see her so, he flung himself across her bed and clutched her tightly, while sobbing uncontrollably. 'P-Please don't leave me, p-please don't leave me Mother.'

'Felix, Felix,' said his mother gently, 'don't get so upset dear, it's just my time, that's all.'

Weakly, she raised a paw, and stroked the side of his face.

Felix continued sobbing.

'One day it will be your time too, and then we can all be together again.'

'But, I want you to s-s-s-stay with me, now,' moaned Felix miserably through his tears. 'Now now, dear,' said Grey Cat softly, 'it's been so very long since your dear father and I were together... and Fergal, Aine and Aoife...' she paused for breath, 'and my own dear mother too of course,' she paused again, 'and I'm wanting to be with them all again, even though it means leaving you...' she paused again to get her breath, '...my best boy.'

Felix gulped and nodded.

'Now you wouldn't want to deny me that, would you?'

Felix shook his head. 'N-No, No,' he said, 'of course not,' and then, arising from the depths of his desperation and despair at the prospect of losing his mother came the words, which, even as he was uttering them, he knew were asking for what was not possible, and could not be granted. 'but can't I come too?' he asked.

His mother's thin body trembled a little from the effort of suppressing a small chuckle which rose from within her.

What a dear boy he was, wanting to be with her, whatever the cost to him. She smiled affectionately at him and said quietly, 'No Felix, now you know that's not the way of things, and cannot be.'

Felix nodded his head, miserably.

'You have a lot more earthly life yet to come and so many more exciting adventures coming your way.' She blinked away a tear, 'And I'm just so, so sorry I have to leave you.'

Felix looked at her intently, the tears streaming down his face.

'But I will be with you, always, watching and minding you… you remember that.'

Grey Cat stopped to get her breath, '…Please don't fret, my darling boy; please don't make this parting any harder than it has to be.' She smiled at him again, 'It breaks my heart too to have to leave you behind you know, but, what has to be, has to be.'

She caught her breath, and continued, hurriedly, 'Please don't be sad for me. We all have to continue our journey at some time or another, and, for some of us, it's sooner than for others… and it's my time now.' Continuing before he could interrupt her, she said, 'I've accepted it and you must too. Now, be a good boy and fetch your Auntie White Cat, I want to speak to her.'

Reluctantly, Felix left his mother's bedside. As he returned with his aunt, his mother asked her to come close so that she could speak to her, and she bade Felix to wait by the door, while she did so.

'My dearest sister,' she said to White Cat, her words then coming quickly and urgently, 'you have always been there for me and never let me down, however bad things became for us, and I will miss you so dreadfully until we meet again, but now I have one last favour to ask of you.' She stopped for breath.

'Anything, anything,' said White Cat softly, the tears rolling slowly down her cheeks as she spoke.

Grey Cat continued, her breath coming in very short gasps as she said, 'I know he is grown up, and so big, but in lots of ways Felix is still very much a kitten.' She stopped and coughed. 'Please, please promise me you will look after him when I'm gone. I know he will be so dreadfully distressed. Please comfort him and watch over him for me in the days to come.'

White Cat nodded, and said, 'Of course, I promise.'

Grey Cat's voice was almost inaudible as she continued, 'You know how he acted when Mary left us, and I'm so afraid he will do or say something silly which could turn away our Lord Provider from looking kindly on him.'

White Cat held up a paw to quieten Grey Cat's anxiety and agitation.

'Please don't worry yourself about Felix,' she said, 'you can rely on me, dearest sister, I will help him through his grief for you. Mori and I know how much he loves you, and it will not be easy for him, but, with our help, he will come through it safely.'

Grey Cat managed to smile weakly, saying, 'Thank you, thank you, that's an enormous weight off my mind.'

White Cat squeezed her sister's paw reassuringly.

The sisters sat quietly for a minute or two, before Grey Cat said, 'Please ask Felix to come back beside me now.'

As Felix approached, Grey Cat struggled to sit up.

'My sweet sister,' she said, hurrying her words, as she was fearful she would not be able to finish what she had to say, 'And my dearest, dearest boy.' Turning her head to smile at Felix, 'It breaks my heart to say goodbye, but it must be so.'

She cradled Felix's head in her arms, and smiling down on him, kissed him gently on the forehead, for the last time.

Then, as she rested her head back on her pillow, she sighed a long sigh and closed her eyes. She knew her work on this earth was done, her destiny was fulfilled, and she was freed now to move on.

And so it was, with her paw clasped tightly in that of her sister, and with her huge son sprawled across her lap, sobbing, Grey Cat meekly and quietly followed the bright light which was beckoning to her, and passed from this world to the next – to where she knew her beloved Horace, her three little ones, her mother, and her little niece, would be waiting to greet her.

White Cat felt her sister's paw relax in hers, and then go limp, and she knew she was gone from them.

Felix was not immediately aware his mother had left them. He was sobbing so loudly and desperately as he clung to his mother's frail, thin little body, and it was as if he was attempting to pass some of his own health and vitality into it, to restore her to health and vitality.

White Cat gently took Felix by the arm. 'She's gone, dear, you have to let her go now.'

'No, no,' sobbed Felix, 'She can't be. She wouldn't leave me, she wouldn't leave me.'

'She had no choice, Felix,' said White Cat softly. 'Our Lord Provider decides when and where we go, and none, not even such as your good, kind mother, can alter that decision.' White Cat turned Felix to face her, and, now sitting so still and quiet, her heart went out to him as he looked at her glumly. He had stopped sobbing, but couldn't stop the tears which still rolled down his cheeks.

His auntie took him in her arms, and, clasping him tightly to her, murmured to him, 'There, there,' and, as she rocked him in her arms as she would a young kitten in distress, 'I know, I know.'

For a long while, Felix buried his face in her fur, in silent misery.

And then, 'She's gone, she's gone.' Felix began to mumble, over and over again. 'I'm all alone now, and what will I do without her?'

'Listen to me now,' said White Cat, 'you're not all alone, you have Mori and me, and we love you,' continuing, 'you have Daisy and Fionn too, and you're going to be fine, a brave boy to make your mother proud of you. She loved you dearly, and still does. She will be with you always – wherever you are, and wherever you go – and so it's up to you now to show her how strong you can be, to deserve the pride and trust she has placed in you.'

Comforted by his aunt's words, Felix thought quietly for a while. His auntie was right.

He had never left home, but now it was his chance to make his mother proud of him… and he would do it, he would surely do it.

White Cat smiled down on Felix's tear stained face as he withdrew his face from her fur, and brushed the tears from his cheeks.

'I *can* be strong,' he said, 'I know I can, and I *will* be worthy of Mother's pride and trust in me.'

'You're a good boy,' said White Cat, 'and it won't be easy for you, but we will do all we can to help you.'

'I loved her so much,' said Felix quietly.

'I know you did, dear,' said White Cat, 'and you still do, and always will.'

She looked wistful. 'I loved her too and will miss her, but…' she said, smiling at Felix through her tears, 'I have you to remind me of the sweetest sister with whom any cat could have been blessed.'

She went on, 'Before you were born, she and I had very hard lives, and it was only the companionship of your dear mother which kept me going. I have a lot to thank her for and I will never forget her.'

Felix was comforted to hear his aunt speaking of his mother with such emotion and gratitude, and he knew then just how much his mother's presence had touched the lives of others, as well as his own, and he was proud to be her son.

Then White Cat took him by the arm again, saying, 'Now, Felix, kiss your mother and come with me to tell Mori the sad news.'

She continued, 'After your father, you were the most important cat in your mother's life, and it should come from you. You are her representative in the family now and it will be you, and only you, who will keep her memory alive.'

Felix realized the importance of the task his aunt had said he must perform. He kissed his mother, looked down lovingly upon her sweet face – so peaceful now – and then followed his aunt out of the barn to join Mori, who was anxiously awaiting news of Grey Cat.

Later on, Felix returned to the barn on his own, to rest his head gently on his mother's chest, and to imagine her arms about him still.

He had not been there long before the door opened. It was Cara, carrying his mother's medicine. When she saw Grey Cat was beyond the help of medication, she lifted Felix gently from his mother's last embrace and hugged him tightly to her. He saw the tears in her eyes and he found it strangely comforting to know that she had loved his mother too.

Cara held him to her for a long time and spoke softly to him in a language he couldn't fully understand, but he knew they were words of sympathy and comfort. He snuggled to her, and wept quietly for his lost mother.

After a long while, Cara set him down and then gently lifted his mother's still form, and wrapped her in her blanket.

The next day, Cara buried her in the soft earth in a sunny corner of the field near the old stone wall of the barn. Felix stood close by, watching, and his tears mingled with the sweet smelling earthen bed which had received his mother's body.

The next year his aunt died – and joined his mother in the sunny corner by the wall.

Horace's Legacy

It was a while after Felix's Auntie White Cat had died, that a messenger from the C.C.C.C. arrived, with a message for Felix to attend a meeting of the Committee that day.

In the time since his mother had died, with the help and support of his aunt, and his cousin, Mori, Felix had matured into a sensible, level-headed adult cat, with a strong sense of family and duty.

Although his happy nature and good-hearted spontaneity remained he had curbed his impulsiveness and had learned the wisdom of a reasoned and measured response to situations beyond his control.

The summons for him to appear before the Committee came as a complete surprise – or shock might be a better description – but he was careful to be polite to the messenger, and followed him to the meeting, without question, or complaint.

He was worried, and didn't know what to expect, but he said nothing.

In truth, Felix was staggered. Surely the fox's family couldn't have complained; that was *years* ago and he had long repented of his actions.

By the time Felix stood before the magistrates, while

he managed to maintain an air of outward calm, inwardly he was quaking, but the only indicator of his agitation was the return of his stutter when he spoke.

Otus spoke first, 'I expect you know why you are here, Felix?' he said.

'It *must* be the fox,' thought Felix, and he started to try to explain the incident with the fox in his youth, and his sincere regret for his behaviour.

Meles and the others laughed. 'No, no Felix, you don't understand, you're not here to be tried by the Committee, you're here to be invited to join it – as a co-opted member…'

'Your inheritance from Horace, your dear father,' interjected Lutra.

When Felix realized just how valued a member of the Committee his father had been, and the respect he had earned for his opinions and reasoning, he was honoured and proud to be his successor, and vowed to do his best to follow his father's example.

'Oh that Mother could see me now,' thought Felix, suppressing a chuckle at the thought of it all being so very different from her stern warning to him, all that time ago, of his appearance before the Committee. 'I guess she didn't know I would inherit father's position… or did she?' wondered Felix. 'Is that why she was so worried the fox would report me?'

From that time on, for the whole of the remainder of his earthly life, Felix served as an exemplary successor to his father on the Committee, showing much of the same capacity for sound advice and judgement.

Goodbye to a Dear Friend

The day Daisy Boxer died was as bad for Felix as those on which his beloved Mary and his dear mother had left him.

She was ill for several days before she died, and, whenever he could, he sneaked in to see and to talk to her.

In spite of feeling so ill and weak, she remained remarkably cheerful. She thanked him for his friendship, and told him that had it not been for him, she couldn't have coped with losing Charlie. He had given her hope, and she was looking forward now to being with Charlie again, who she knew was waiting for her.

The promise Felix made to Daisy on the day Charlie died had indeed already been fulfilled when, from his hiding place in the bushes, he watched her earthly body lowered gently and carefully into the soft earth beside Charlie's grave.

Silently, he whispered goodbye to her.

The tears for her flowed down his cheeks, but he was content; he knew that in their place beyond the end of the rainbow, she and Charlie were together again, for ever.

He thought of Daisy, now in Newlife, and imagined the joy of her reunion with Charlie. He was so happy for her – his dear friend – and for Charlie too. Silently he wished them every joy of their eternal happiness together, a happiness which they both so richly deserved.

He would miss his dear friend dreadfully, but now he had another job to do for her, to comfort poor Fionn, who was alone now and was grieving for her too.

Korky

Until Korky entered his life, all the cats and kittens who had come and gone over the years were quite unlike Felix in appearance.

For a while now, on Felix's daily strolls down to the pond, over the rock bridge, and on to the honeysuckle walk, and thence to the seashore beyond, he had become conscious of being observed from the surrounding bushes.

At first he dismissed the feeling as nonsense, but, as it persisted, he became more and more convinced that he was being watched.

One sunny Autumn afternoon, the feeling was stronger than ever and he decided to investigate: He continued his walk along the honeysuckle walk, but then, at the point the path dipped down out of a direct line of sight, he doubled back and crept silently, under the cover of the ferns alongside the path, to return to the point where he had felt those unknown eyes upon him.

Felix's heart was thumping with excitement and he had to stifle a giggle, as this creeping along, keeping out of sight, was so reminiscent of the stalking games of his kittenhood.

Then he saw him. A tiny black and white kitten, and so very like himself in appearance, especially at that age.

Felix circled around behind the stranger, crept forward silently, and then said, 'Hello, I'm Felix, and who might you be?'

The streak of a sense of mischief still in Felix in his dotage was delighted with the effect. The kitten leapt into the air on the spot. Fright had caused every hair on his tiny body to stand up, and he looked so very like a cartoon cat that, once again, Felix had to stifle a giggle.

The kitten landed back on to his feet and appeared rooted to the spot, with his only movement being to turn his huge, dark eyes towards Felix, and regard him with abject terror.

Instantly, the good-hearted Felix regretted his practical joke upon this terrified little creature.

'Calm down,' he said, 'I'm not going to hurt you.'

There was no response from the kitten.

He continued, 'All I want to know is who you are and what you're doing here.'

The kitten still said nothing, and continued to stare at Felix. It was then that Felix noticed he was trembling.

'Come on now,' said Felix, 'there's no need to get upset.'

He regarded the kitten more closely and saw he was in very bad condition. He was painfully thin and his coat was ragged and dirty. Quite obviously, during his short life, he had been living rough.

Felix wondered why he was away from his mother at such a young age, and where was the rest of his family?

He tried again.

'Now, now,' he said, 'you just relax and tell me all about it,' and, to his immense surprise and some embarrassment, the kitten burst into tears, and, between sobs, tried to tell his story.

Still being so young, his account was garbled, but Felix listened patiently and eventually was able to elicit the gist of what had happened to this lonely, distressed little creature. He was born the only kitten of a very young and inexperienced mother. He had never known any of her family, or his father, or his father's family. There had just been his mother. He loved her and she loved him, keeping him close and warm.

He thought she was not in very good health, because she coughed a lot, and sometimes had difficulty in producing enough milk for him, but they were together, and that's all that mattered. He was sure she was the most beautiful cat in all the world and his eyes shone with his love and admiration for his dearest 'Mamma'.

They had lived in the bushes nearby, in a hollow beneath the exposed roots of an old whitethorn tree. His mother had told him it was the driest and warmest place she could find for him.

Although he was always hungry, whenever the milk stopped when he was suckling, he had told his mother he had had enough and was full. As he grew, his mother brought him what solid food she could find and he believed she was giving virtually all of it to him. She looked very thin. Then, one night, he thought about five or six cat weeks ago, she had not come back to him. He had waited, and waited, and still there was no sign of her.

At this point in the little one's story, Felix remembered a screech of vehicle brakes on the lane beside the neighbouring field, which had been around that time, and of seeing evidence on the road the next morning of a collision between a vehicle and one of their kind, but he said nothing.

The kitten continued, telling him how he hadn't known what to do. If he left the home his mother had made for him in order to look for her, he was worried she would return in his absence and think he had left her, but, if he stayed, he would starve.

He had decided on a compromise, and had stayed within ear-shot of his home, while searching in ever-widening circles to try to find his mother. He had not found her. He had watched Felix because he had been trying to pluck up the courage to ask him if he had seen his mother, but had been too frightened to do so after having already asked one passing big black male cat, who had ignored his question, and then attacked him, telling him to 'Clear off' and that he was not wanted there.

The kitten showed Felix the deep scratches and bites he had had inflicted upon his thin little body, and Felix noticed how badly the edges of both of his ears had been torn. He just wished he had been around at the time to deal with the bully who had injured this defenceless baby so badly.

'Well,' said Felix, 'I think you had best come home with me.' He smiled at the kitten. 'I'm sure Cara can fix you up and get some food into you.'

The kitten's eyes shone with gratitude. 'Thank you, thank you so much,' he said, and then added quietly, 'I guess I'm not going to see Mamma again, am I?'

His lip was trembling and his eyes pleaded to be reassured that no ill had befallen his beloved mother.

His eyes then filled with tears, and he began to cry again.

'Well,' said Felix hastily, 'wherever she is just now, I'm sure she's thinking of you, so, tell you what, why don't we leave her a message at your home, so she'll know where to come to find you.'

'Oh, yes, yes,' said the kitten, 'I don't want her to think I've left her.'

The kitten dried his tears and then, smiling happily, he set off eagerly, skipping along ahead of Felix to guide him to his home.

When they arrived, the kitten showed Felix the hollow beneath the exposed roots of a gnarled old whitethorn tree and said shyly, 'This is where Mamma and I live. This is my home.'

While Felix showed him how to leave unmistakable marks and signs that his mother would be able to read to know to where he had gone, he thought about the kitten's mother.

He knew she would never willingly have left him on his own at so young an age and so undoubtedly she had been the road accident victim. By now she would have entered Newlife, beyond the end of the rainbow, and no longer in a position to care for her beloved kitten. It was as well though that the little one didn't know that, and had hope of seeing his mother again. As he grew older, it would be easier for him to accept the truth.

Felix could only imagine the depth of anguish of that young mother, as she lay dying, knowing that her young kitten was alone and helpless without her. Silently, he prayed to their Lord Provider for her to know that her baby had found a friend, who would protect him, and care for him.

He looked sadly upon the humble little home that tragic young mother had made for herself and her kitten. They had been happy there and it was so cruel of fate to have parted them.

Felix's thoughts fleeted back to his beloved Mary, and the pain of their parting, but no, he thought, there was work to do, and he forced his thoughts back to the present – to the tiny kitten sitting quietly at his feet, looking up at him expectantly, waiting for instructions.

He cleared his throat and said, 'Well, we had best be off – it's nearly teatime and we don't want to miss that, do we?'

The kitten shook his head and smiled happily.

'Oh, by the way,' said Felix, 'what is your name?'

'Mamma called me Korky,' said the kitten.

And so it was that, as the sun was setting, two figures set off together along the honeysuckle walk, heading for home.

Ahead, showing the way, was the large, imposing black and white bulk of Felix, and trotting along behind, chattering non-stop in his excitement, a tiny black and white kitten of almost identical markings to his benefactor. Korky had joined the family!

The Felcans

Korky coming into his life made all the difference to the ageing Felix, who, more and more of late, had been inclined to spend his time in quiet contemplation of the past, remembering, with sadness of their having ended, the days of the hustle, bustle and fun of having his family around him.

It was so good to have a youngster around the place again, and, for him, Korky now re-kindled all the joy he had known as 'Uncle Felix' to young Mori and Arti, and, this time, he knew that his protégé was here to stay.

Korky was such a little dote, he had touched Cara's heart. She had become very attached to him, and, after all he had been through, Felix knew he would never be expected to leave to go to a new home.

Korky would become the son he had never had, and Felix was determined to raise him to be his successor. Being so like him in appearance, it made it easy for Felix to begin to think of Korky as his son.

In no time at all, from a skinny kitten, very small for his age, Korky began to fill out and to grow a little, and it was not too long before he was fit enough to start his education.

As he had done, long, long ago, with young Mori and Arti, Felix conducted Korky around his home and regaled him with all the stories of his own kittenhood.

Even cricket was back on the agenda, albeit having to be played under amended rules because of the lack of other players. With just the three of them – Felix, Fionn and Korky – it was difficult, but they managed to come up with a version which was nearly as much fun and which kept alive the competitive spirit from the old days when always there had been more than enough wanting to play, because of having more family, and lots of friends and neighbours around, all only too happy to join the teams.

Felix and Korky took turns at batting – with the other bowling – and Fionn was content to be permanent fielder for both sides. He was an expert with a ball and fielded for both sides with equal enthusiasm, showing no favouritism to either.

Having gained considerably in weight since the days of cricket on family picnics, it was quite an effort for Felix to run between the wickets, but, as he had of old, he put his all into the matches, and, in the manner of those of portly stature, was surprisingly fleet on his feet. His determination was matched by Korky's youth, and, with Fionn's skill with a ball being applied equally to both sides, most usually the matches were declared a draw, and so everyone ended up tired, but happy.

They called themselves 'The Felcans'.

Sometimes as they played, Felix fancied he saw the shadowy figures of his family, watching and waiting at their game, but he didn't tell the other two. If indeed his family was there, he was content, and hoped they enjoyed the matches as much as he did. In particular, he hoped his dearest mother approved of his adopted son, and the way in which he was raising him. He wanted her to be proud of her own son, and of the youngster who had come to fill the place of her grandson.

Korky and Fionn remained blissfully unaware of Felix's thoughts of his family.

As time passed, Korky blossomed into a handsome young cat, with a fine physique and glossy coat.

Felix swelled with pride to see him.

Korky was an apt pupil and of a most affable disposition and so, for Felix, teaching him was a pleasure.

During his lessons, he was always polite and attentive and Felix was sure that Korky's dearest mamma would have been so proud of him.

As he grew older, Korky came to accept the loss of his mother, but, every now and then, the pain of losing her would come to the fore again.

At those times, he would slip away quietly and return to his old home beneath the whitethorn tree, and there shed tears for her.

His intent was to conceal these episodes from Felix, because he didn't want to appear ungrateful for all he had been given, and had had done for him, in Felix's home.

Felix was an ageing cat, now wise in the ways of the world, and always he recognized the signs of Korky missing his mother, watching him from a distance as he made his pilgrimage back to his old home, where he felt close to her. When Korky returned, Felix would talk to him quietly about missing his own family – which comforted Korky to know he was not alone in missing his mother – and then would suggest some boisterous fun activity to cheer him.

Felix's approach to Korky's grief for his mother never failed to comfort and cheer the youngster.

After the trauma of finding himself alone at such a young age, Korky thanked Felix, and their Lord Provider, for guiding him to safe sanctuary, and wished that all little kittens suffering in similar circumstances could be so blessed. 'The Felcans' continued with just three players, until Korky befriended Mr Mac. Mr Mac had been abandoned by his people when they had moved away. He was very happy to be drafted into 'The Felcans' as permanent wicket-keeper to both sides.

End of an Era

Felix was feeling his age. More and more of late, he found his thoughts dwelling in the past, upon those halcyon days when he had all his immediate family around him.

Apart from himself, there was only old Fionn left now from those days. It was after Mori had left him that he had really begun to feel his age.

He remembered how, at the time he had found Korky, he had wished so much she had still been around to lend a hand with him.

As a past mother of young kittens herself, her help would have been invaluable to him in those early days of rearing such a very young kitten, who was so desperately missing his own mother.

He sighed as he thought of Mori. Like him, she too had been blessed with an exceptionally long life, she eventually leaving this world while sleeping peacefully in her bed.

She had been of his generation, and he not only missed her company and companionship very much, he felt too that her loss had marked the end of an era in his family's history, and so that was now lost to him too.

He felt happy for her though, knowing that, in Newlife, the awkwardness which had persisted between her and his Auntie White Cat in life, would have dispersed there as quickly and as easily as an early morning mist over what was to become a beautiful sunny day. He knew that she and Auntie White Cat would be close again now, just as a mother and daughter ought to be.

And what of Maxi and Pepper? Were they still alive? He had no way of knowing, but he was content in the certain knowledge that one day he would meet up with them again too.

Going Home

Felix sat quietly, enjoying the late June sunshine, while he watched Korky and Mr Mac play boxing.

He was so proud to see the way in which Korky, his protégé, had developed. Such a fine young adult. His sleek, well-groomed coat shone in the sunlight, its dense black colour accentuated by the snowy white of mask, chest and stockings. Felix beamed his approval.

It was almost unbelievable that, from the little scrap of a thing he had been when he had found him, by some miracle, he had managed to grow into the handsome young cat now before him.

Korky had a fine physique, and muscles now rippled where once there had been just the scraggy skin and bone of a tiny malnourished frame.

Kind, thoughtful and generous, Korky's disposition was as admirable as his physique. Although, eventually, he had lost the timidness of the hungry, lost kitten Felix had found, he had never forgotten the bad experiences of his early kittenhood, immediately empathizing with others who were homeless and in distress.

Mr Mac was one who had reason to be grateful to Korky – for noticing his predicament, when his people had moved house and left him behind. Korky had been sure Mr Mac would be welcomed into the home he now shared with Felix and dog friend, Fionn, and had taken Mr Mac to meet them.

True to Korky's word, Mr Mac was welcomed into the family and, being only a little older than Korky, quickly he and Korky became inseparable, and, in all but name, were as brothers.

Felix was content. He felt he might allow himself some credit for the way in which Korky had turned out, and he was delighted to see him now with the company of a companion of a comparable age. He hoped the two would remain lifelong friends.

He turned to look at his old friend, Fionn. He thought of the lonely, distressed puppy he had comforted when Daisy Boxer died. He sighed; all such a long, long time ago now.

Undeniably, his friend was ageing, spending more and more of his time day-dreaming, or sleeping, the days away. Felix looked on his friend, as he lay sleeping, with his huge old head and neck draped down across his front legs and paws, the all grey muzzle twitching to the dictates of his adventures in a private world of dreams.

Felix knew he too was ageing fast now, and it saddened him to witness the zeal and energy – with which he had always lived his life – ebbing slowly, but inexorably, away. He was a very old cat now, and he was tired.

He was always tired these days and his great appetite was not what it was – even tempting titbits were a disappointment to him once they were in his mouth. He had always loved his food, and yet now somehow it all seemed bland and tasteless after one or two mouthfuls. What was happening to him?

There were other changes in him too which he couldn't explain.

Although he was so tired, of late he had felt a restlessness, which would not be stilled. He felt drawn to the seashore.

Always he had taken a stroll along the seashore when the weather was fine, and the fancy took him, but this was different. This was a mission, feeling it was something set for him to do by destiny. He felt a sense of urgency and that there was someone, or something waiting there for him to find, but he had no idea who, or what, it might be, or where on the seashore he would find it, but find it he would.

From daybreak until late into the evening he could be found pacing the seashore, ever searching.

Most nights as darkness fell, Cara would come down to the shore, calling his name, and he would be happy then for her to carry him back home and put him to bed.

The next day though, he would be back there again. He was a cat with a mission. Felix sighed again. He felt tired, but maybe a stroll before teatime would revive his spirits.

He stood up and looked around, first at his old and dear friend, Fionn, still fast asleep in the sunshine, and then at his two dear lads, still boisterously sparring, and laughing all the while they bobbed and weaved before each other.

He looked long and hard at this scene of his remaining family, inexplicably feeling that he had to meticulously commit every bit of it to memory now, for fear this could be the last time he saw the three in the world who were dearest to him.

Shaking himself to cast off the thoughts of having to

leave them one day, unnoticed, he slipped away for his stroll in the sunshine.

As he passed by the pyramid stone, on over the rock bridge and onto the honeysuckle walk, thoughts of Fionn, Korky, and Mr Mac retreated to the back of his mind, and, as he walked, he pondered on whether today might be the day he would find whatever it was he was so urgently seeking.

On reaching the gate out onto the seashore, he noticed the bay was bathed in an unusual muted golden light.

He shaded his eyes against the sun, and, far in the distance along the sandy shore, he fancied he could see shadowy figures. He thought he could make out five, but it was difficult to be certain, because they drifted in and out of that peculiar light and, just as he thought he had fixed his failing eyesight on the group, they were gone again.

It was all very odd.

He stayed on the seashore for some time. There was .something familiar to him about those figures, but they were never close enough for him to see their number clearly, or who they might be.

Fatigue from pursuing the shadowy figures, as they appeared in the distance, and then disappeared again as he approached, finally overtook Felix and he decided to call it a day.

On this particular day, as the sun had risen higher and higher in the sky, it had become hotter and hotter, and the heat from its rays still shimmered above the grey pebbles on the upper shore. The white sand which began closer to the sea was still warm to the pads of his paws, and, squinting his eyes against the shimmering surface of the blue water of the bay, he felt very hot. Indefatigable as he was, he *had* to rest.

He made his way back across the sand, tiptoed lightly and quickly across the still hot pebbles, and, to get his breath back, he sat for a few minutes on the rocks which fringed the seashore, before slowly making his way up to the gate by the big whitethorn tree.

He was glad his age had slimmed his body sufficiently to be able to just squeeze through the gate's bars, because, if the only way nowadays had been to have to jump over it, he would have been forced to spend the night on the beach! He thought again of his youth, to a time when he would have jumped back and forth over the gate, just for fun.

Once through the bars, he needed another rest in the cool glade behind the gate, before tackling the flights of steps which led up the bank and onto the honeysuckle walk. He was heading for his favourite spot – the pyramid stone.

As he started up the steps, he looked back towards the bay and thought of their Lord Provider, the Giver of Life, blessing cats and all other creatures with such a truly beautiful world in which to live.

Then he frowned, and, as he had so many times in the past, he wondered why humans were so intent upon destroying it. The oddity of human behaviour captured his attention, thinking that, as a species, they must be exceptionally stupid and ignorant to destroy what they depended upon for their own survival. It made no sense. It was a great mystery to him as to why humans should have assumed a place they considered to be above that of their fellow creatures. 'They can do lots of things we can't of course,' he thought, 'but none of the rest of us is as daft as they in the things that really matter; the things we know instinctively.'

As ever, any answers to the mysteries of human behaviour eluded him completely and he brought his thoughts back to the task in hand and continued on his way.

By the time he reached the pond beyond the other end of the honeysuckle walk, he was exhausted.

He rested again, and, as always, he was cheered as he watched the large electric-blue dragonflies and the smaller red damselflies as they darted and hovered above the surface of the still water and the cool rushes, amid the fluttering of the brightly coloured butterflies and the droning of very busy bees as they made their way from flower to flower at the water's edge.

He felt good now, but so, so tired. 'One final effort though,' he thought, 'and I'll be home in time for tea.'

He stood up, crossed the rock bridge and began up the slope towards the barn, but, when abreast of the pyramid stone, he felt just too tired to go any further.

There it was, he thought, his place.

Sitting down, beside his stone on its shadier side, immediately he enjoyed at his back the residual warmth of that face of the huge stone, gathered from the heat of the sun's rays on its surface earlier in the day.

He sighed contentedly, and gently slid his body down, to stretch out full length against the base of the stone. He rested his head on a convenient tussock of grass, and there, listening to the fluttering of the ivy leaves on the stone behind his head, he gave a long sigh, and began to give himself up to drift off into heavenly sleep.

'Perfect,' thought Felix drowsily, 'almost as comfortable as my own bed… I'll rest a while here,' and then, 'Hope I'll still be in time for tea though.'

In the land of dreams, Felix smiled as he slept. He was happy. He was dreaming of Mary, of his mother, of Arti and Mori Junior, and of the happy days of his kittenhood.

He re-visited the family outings and picnics; he was savouring every blissful minute of them again. The happy chatter and the laughter. The excitement of the hamper of food being opened, to discover what his mother and Auntie White Cat had decided to bring that day to tempt their appetites, and then, when eaten outside in the fresh air and sunshine, even the simplest of fare became a feast.

On hot days, there would be the welcome flask of cool water to drink, and then it would be Mori Junior and Arti who would be most in need of it, to repeatedly slake their thirst as they ran about, playing happily in the sunshine.

It was always with great reluctance that the two kittens did their mother's bidding and sat (fidgeting) in the shade for a while, when she was becoming anxious that they might be overheating and could be in danger of getting sunstroke. Just as soon though as they had cooled down again, and were allowed to do so, they would be away once more, running hither and thither, like two tiny indomitable March hares.

Wonderful, wonderful times. And of course the cricket. He could see Arti and Mori Junior running towards him, holding their bats and ball, eyes shining with excitement.

'Uncle Felix, Uncle Felix,' they pleaded, 'come and play cricket with us.'

Always he had feigned reluctance, but, in truth, always he had been waiting, almost anxiously, to be asked.

Once they had 'persuaded' him to join in, he played with such gusto that, in the company of his two tiny companions, he became a huge, overgrown kitten, hitting as hard, and running as fast, as his huge bulk would allow.

Eventually, when totally out of breath from the effort, he would fling himself back down on the grass to recover, when the two kittens would then sit close beside him, to go over and over who bowled out whom, who fell over trying to field the ball, who tripped over the wickets, etc., etc. Always in Uncle Felix's company, they were epic games of drama and excitement.

He was not their uncle of course, but he flushed with pleasure every time they addressed him so, and he entered into his honorary avuncular role with such enthusiasm, often he forgot that they were not actually his niece and nephew. He adored them, and they adored him.

Such were the happy memories of bygone days filling Felix's dreams as he slept on.

The sun was setting when they found him.

Cara touched him gently and spoke softly to him.

'Come along, Felix,' she said, 'it's past time for your tea, and you don't want to miss that, now do you?'

He didn't stir.

She touched him again, and then cried out, 'Oh no.'

She turned to Abe, saying, 'He's gone, and, after all

these years together, I wasn't with him when it happened.'

'Well, you know you couldn't be with him every minute of every day,' said Abe, 'and, just look at him, lying there so peaceful and content.'

Cara picked up Felix and cradled him in her arms.

Abe continued, 'There you can see he's just fallen asleep, and it was his time, so nature took its course and he just didn't wake up again,' he paused, 'and that's a wonderful way for him to go.'

Cara nodded.

'And, knowing Felix, you can bet that wherever he is now, he's making the most of it and is really happy.'

'I hope so,' murmured Cara, 'I hope so.'

Later that evening, when she carried Felix's old lifeless body across the yard, Cara looked down upon him.

His still form looked so peaceful as he lay there, carefully wrapped in his favourite blanket, and with a tiny piece of folded tissue paper clasped in one paw.

She had found the little package under his pillow, and, knowing he must have treasured it for some reason, she had placed it in his paw, to take with him on his final journey. As she then stood by his grave, and stroked his old greying head for the last time, she was sure he was smiling. She whispered a fond farewell to an old and very dear friend and bade him safe journey, before lowering him gently into the soft earth – in the shade of the pink hydrangea bush, where, all those years before, he had seen his beloved Mary laid to rest.

Epilogue

As the soft blanket of sleep began to lift from him, Felix fancied he heard his mother's voice.

'Felix,' she called softly, 'come along dear, it's time to go now.'

Felix felt good, very good, in fact he felt better than he had felt for a long time. He was refreshed. That sleep really had done him the world of good.

Once fully awake, he looked around him and saw that he was still by the pyramid stone where he had fallen asleep earlier, but also he had the oddest feeling that he wasn't there.

All very peculiar, but, at the same time, exciting, and strangely comforting. He looked down at his thick sleek coat and flexed his legs and arms.

'I must be dreaming,' he thought, 'I feel and look so young again.' He yawned widely, and stretched again.

Then he got up, and, forgetting all about his tea, he trotted down to the pond, across the rock bridge, fairly scampered off down the honeysuckle walk to the glade, and then back through the gate.

It was then that he saw them.

His dearest mother, with a handsome cat at her side whom he knew to be his father, and, holding hands in front of them, were Fergal, Aine and Aoife. He knew then he had fulfilled his destiny.

Felix looked back in the direction of his earthly home, which was fast disappearing from sight in a swirling mist.

He thought of Cara and whispered, 'Thank you for loving me.' He blinked away a tear. 'I have loved you too, but it's time now for me to go home.'

Although Cara hadn't had the advantage of a feline education, he hoped she could understand.

Then, he turned away, and, without another backward glance, he faced into the wind, fixed his gaze firmly upon his dear family in the distance, and set off towards them as fast as his new young legs could carry him.

As he collided with them, his father laughed indulgently and said, 'Really, Felix, you don't change much, do you?' and there, with all the others crowded around him, and everyone talking at once, his mother threw her arms about him and clasped him to her tightly.

She was sobbing with joy, and all he could make out of what she was saying to him through her tears, was, 'My beautiful, beautiful boy.' He was on his way home.

Far, far away, beyond the end of the rainbow, two small kittens waited expectantly, excitedly clutching their bats and ball, and an exquisitely beautiful young girl cat looked up from the picnic spread out on the green pasture, and smiled. She knew her long wait was over. Her handsome young fiancé was on his way to her, at last.

THE END